THE GIRL WHO DREAMED IN MAGIC

Maria Kuzniar

PUFFIN

PUFFIN BOOKS

UK | USA | Canada | Ireland | Australia
India | New Zealand | South Africa

Puffin Books is part of the Penguin Random House group of companies
whose addresses can be found at global.penguinrandomhouse.com.

www.penguin.co.uk
www.puffin.co.uk
www.ladybird.co.uk

First published 2024

001

Set in 11/16.5pt Sabon LT Std
Typeset by Jouve (UK), Milton Keynes
Printed and bound in Great Britain by Clays Ltd, Elcograf S.p.A.

The authorized representative in the EEA is Penguin Random House Ireland,
Morrison Chambers, 32 Nassau Street, Dublin D02 YH68

A CIP catalogue record for this book is available from the British Library

ISBN: 978–0–241–62466–1

All correspondence to:
Puffin Books
Penguin Random House Children's
One Embassy Gardens, 8 Viaduct Gardens, London SW11 7BW

For Paul Kuzniar, who will always be my little brother,
even though you're now much taller than me!

SAGA'S VILLAGE

RUVSÁ'S WINTER CAMP

THE WITCH'S
CAVE

BIFROST

THE SORCERERS' ICE CASTLE

THE FAR NORTH

CANUTE'S VILLAGE

NORVEGR

PROLOGUE

One day, some years ago, a seer walked into a village. The village had been carved out between mountains and sea, on lands that were born on the winds of magic. As the seer passed through, her staff thumping into the snow, people stepped back, afraid of her power.

It was said that she could see a thousand years into the future and could tell you the day you'd die ... whether you wanted to know or not.

Just beyond the village square, she stopped before a wooden house shaped like a ship, and when she knocked on the door of the longhouse with her staff it opened with a creak. A tall man stood in the doorway, taking in her clouded eyes and hands gnarled like roots. He nodded sadly. 'I knew she was special,' he murmured.

The seer made her way over to a fire crackling and spitting in the centre of the room. On a fur before the flames lay a baby and a bear cub, curled up together like two crescent moons.

The seer peered down at them milkily. 'The seers speak of a girl,' she said. 'A girl braver than a raider and fiercer than an eagle, who will ride a bear over the tundra during the dayless night.'

The man watched as his baby granddaughter opened her eyes and smiled up at him, her gaze as blue as the oldest glacier. 'You have a magical destiny, Saga,' he told her, filled with pride and worry.

The seer turned to leave.

'Wait,' called out Saga's grandfather. 'Why have you come to tell us this?'

The seer hesitated before the door. 'The girl will dream magic.' Her lined face drooped. 'And she holds the fate of the North in her hands.'

PART ONE
THE VILLAGE

The village had been carved out between mountains and sea, on lands that were born on the winds of magic.

CHAPTER ONE
A MAGICAL DESTINY

'Bjørn, no!' Saga Thorolfsdottir laughed as her brown bear lumbered over to the cauldron on the fire. It was breakfast time inside their cosy longhouse, and Saga was twelve years old today. She'd been left in charge of the porridge while her grandfather fetched a mystery present from his little workshop next door.

Bjørn looked at her, then back at the cauldron filled with the porridge he was particularly fond of. Slowly, he lifted a paw.

Saga narrowed her eyes at him. '*Bjørn.*'

With a playful snuffle, Bjørn dipped his paw into the cauldron.

Saga squealed, 'No!' The last time they'd had porridge, Bjørn had accidentally tipped the whole cauldron over in his excitement and it had taken *days* to get all of the clumps out of his fur.

But this time Bjørn huffed cheekily and waved his paw – his *clean* paw – at Saga, delighted that she'd fallen for his teasing.

Saga giggled.

The longhouse door thudded open. Snow flurried around Saga's grandfather, who stood there dressed in furs, his hair tied back above his silvering beard. He grunted as he carried something large and wooden inside.

'There,' he said proudly, standing the sledge next to their table. 'I have finished.' His bright blue eyes twinkled at her.

'Thank you, Afi.' Saga ran over and hugged him, breathing in the smell of the tundra and forest on his furs. She had grown up on stories of her afi's bravery, how he had sailed to distant lands and battled other clans that lived in the North. But there had been no more of that since Saga's parents had died. Now the only wars he fought were against the wood he shaped into wonderful things for the village, and instead of spending his days at sea he spent them with Saga. It was funny to hear of her afi being a fierce warrior when he had the kindest eyes she'd ever seen.

Saga examined her new sledge eagerly, already excited to try it out. It had carved wooden runners that would fly over the snow, and it was reinforced with iron to make it strong enough for her bear to sit on too. She ran her hands over it, but when her touch reached a tiny engraving, she pulled back as if she'd been bitten.

'Saga,' her grandfather began, 'you cannot avoid the runes forever. It is time to –'

'The porridge will be done now,' she interrupted, walking back to the fire.

She knew what he was going to say. Runes were a gift from Odin, the one-eyed god of wisdom and magic. They were tools – ways to channel magic. But, when used by the right person, they could be unbelievably powerful. Over the years, Afi had taught Saga all kinds of useful things – like how to start a fire in the snow, how to fight with a sword and how to make the tastiest porridge – but she'd never let him teach her how to use magic.

Saga's mind flew back to the day when the trolls had last lumbered over the mountains and stormed their little village. Saga had been just five. She remembered hearing screams and hiding under the table as her parents turned to the runes to defend the village. The magic of the runes tore through their longhouse with a great ice-bright *whoosh*, splintering the wooden walls and turning little Saga's hair silver.

The trolls were blasted away yet the magic soared on, gathering and growing, until the entire village was protected by a shimmering shield of magic. It glimmered from mountaintop to mountaintop, leaving only a secret sliver open in the harbour. A doorway for boats to sail through. No trolls had been able to invade since; the shield remained in place to this day.

But Saga's parents had not survived channelling such great power. And, though Saga couldn't remember them dying, whenever she thought of magic it was tangled up with the horror of that day and the details that had somehow stuck in her memory: the cracking of wood as their longhouse was split open and the stench of the trolls. She had vowed to the gods that she would never carve a single rune. Shuddering, she kept her head turned from the sledge – and the rune for safe travel that her grandfather had engraved on it.

Bjørn snuffled at her sympathetically, patting her back with a paw as she ladled out porridge into three bowls, two small, one large. She drizzled honey on top and placed the bowls on the low pine table. Her grandfather had shucked off his furs and was sitting, watching her silently. Saga started eating her porridge, sweet and sticky, not sure what to say. She told her afi almost everything; there was nobody better to cheer her up with a story or sort out her problems with his wise advice, but lately this old argument kept rearing up between them, attacking their conversations with teeth and claws. Saga didn't like it one bit. They were all the family each other had. Except for Bjørn.

Saga rested one hand on her bear's side, his fur comforting and warm, making her feel better right away. Their little family of three might look a bit different to other families, but for Saga they were her home and, though she sometimes missed her parents, she couldn't imagine life any differently.

Bjørn dunked his nose into his larger bowl and began slurping. Saga giggled. When she glanced at her grandfather, his mouth twitched. But it wasn't long before he pushed his bowl away and sighed. 'You are twelve years of age today, Saga. You must learn to battle this fear against magic.'

Saga's heart filled with frost. Some days it felt as if magic was soaked into the land itself, from the runes scattered around her small village, to the sorcerers that lived in their ice castle in the islands of the Far North, ruling from the source of magic and guarding Bifrost, the burning rainbow bridge that led to the world of the gods. It was getting harder and harder to avoid it. To everybody else, magic was wondrous and exciting. But for Saga it was the stuff of nightmares.

'We can start small,' her afi continued, pulling his knife from the scabbard he wore, strapped across his right shoulder. He dug the blade into the table and carved a rune for protection.

Saga could hear it, humming through the wood. She stood up, shaking her head. The sound seemed to rattle her bones and she turned cold with fear.

'No, I don't want to.'

Her grandfather stood too. 'If you do not practise, there will come a day when you wish you had,' he said. 'Do not forget –'

'I know – you keep telling me that I have a magical destiny.' Saga's voice cracked like sea ice. 'But I don't want it.'

She ran to the door, pausing only to snatch up her furs and her skates before fleeing outside. 'I never have!'

CHAPTER TWO
THE FIFTH WINTER

Saga stomped through the snow towards the harbour. She found the little longboat that her afi had made her on her last birthday, and climbed inside. Silvery fish slipped in and out of the ripples like fallen stars. A ring of mountains cradled the fjord, their steep walls of rock coated with snow. Here and there, an eagle cried out in the distance and the air was thick with salt. Saga propped her chin up on her arms as she watched the lantern-lit morning boats glide out of the harbour and into deeper, colder water, where the secret doorway through the magical shield lay. When they returned, the fisherfolk's eyelashes would be frozen and their nets heaving with fish. Behind her, the wooden buildings of the village were cosy with firelight, but Saga's mood was as gloomy as the black skies. Suddenly, her end of the little boat leaped up into the air. She held on to the wooden bench and laughed. 'Bjørn!'

Her bear, now sitting on the other side of the boat, tilted his head to one side and cocked an ear, listening. 'You nearly made me fall in!' Saga continued before spotting her best friend, Dag, and waving at him. They'd become best friends the day that Dag had pulled a thorn out of Bjørn's paw, and they'd had many adventures since, skating, sledding and exploring as far as they could under the shield.

He came over at once, wearing a giant hat that hid his black hair and kept falling down to his pink nose. 'Saga, what are you doing down here?'

'I fought with Afi,' Saga told him glumly.

Bjørn whined. He could sense Saga's moods and hated it when she was sad or upset.

Dag scrunched up his nose in sympathy. 'Was it about the runes again?'

Saga nodded.

'Don't worry, you'll make up. You always do.' Dag gave her a reassuring smile. 'Everyone's skating up at the lake, do you want to go?'

Saga picked up her skates and vaulted over the side of the boat. Her leather boots had been waterproofed with fish oil so that she could splash through the shallow water without getting her feet wet. She picked up a torch that had been left, dug into the stones on the shoreline, still flaming bright. 'Let's go!'

Guided by the fiery torchlight, the two children rode Bjørn over the tundra, his paws crunching through glittering snow, until they reached a small lake on the outskirts of their village. Deep in the heart of a hundred fir trees, the lake was milky-white, its thick ice glistening. There, they strapped their bone skates to the soles of their boots and stepped on to the lake.

Bjørn sniffed distastefully at the ice, curling up at the side of the lake to keep a watchful eye on Saga and Dag as they found their skating feet.

Half the village seemed to be out on the lake, with a group of younger children playing nearby. One of them slipped and fell head over heels on the ice, making the others laugh. Saga leaped up, ready to rush over to help, until she saw the expression on the boy's face. He wasn't hurt, but a telltale blush was creeping up his cheeks. He shouted, 'You won't be laughing when I enter the contest, will you?'

The children dissolved into giggles again, and one girl stepped forward, rolling her eyes. 'You, enter the contest? Now that I *would* like to see!'

The boy stood up and regained his balance on the ice. 'Well, then you'll *love* seeing me win and get all the magic in the land!' He stuck out his tongue and the girl gave him a playful nudge.

Saga snorted. Dag gave her a curious look as the pair strayed out further from the torchlight, where the ice was as dark as the night sky.

'What?' Saga asked.

'Do you know what year it is?' Dag's grey eyes shone brighter than moonlight. 'It's the Fifth Winter.'

'Already?' Saga frowned. Their village was one of many scattered around the north of Norvegr, but if you voyaged further still, across a perilous sea to the frozen islands in the Far North, you would find the sorcerers. According to legend, the sorcerers were so powerful that they crackled with magic, and their special magically forged tools were the only ones that could prise ice crystals out of the stone that was found deep down on their islands.

Pure, raw magic came from the Northern Lights, giving everyone who lived under its light magical abilities, but a long time ago a sorcerer had discovered that if you distilled the Northern Lights into an ice crystal, it would amplify the magic of whoever held the crystal, until ordinary people were nearly as powerful as a sorcerer. But when the sorcerers held one, they didn't only wield incredible magic – they were like gods.

The sorcerers were meant to rule over the North, but Saga didn't know anyone who had ever met a sorcerer. Each village had its own Jarl to keep things running smoothly and if there was a bigger problem the sorcerers sent down a couple of ice crystals. But the power of the crystals didn't last long. Saga had only seen one ice crystal before – it was embedded in the hilt of her afi's axe and it had run out of magic long ago, drained in battle. If you wanted more, you would have to enter the Fifth Winter.

The Fifth Winter was a contest the sorcerers held every five winters and the only way you were allowed inside their castle. The first fifty contestants to enter the doors were allowed to compete and the winner received a horn filled with ice crystals.

When Saga had asked Afi why the sorcerers hosted the Fifth Winter, he had told her that they were lazy rulers, and their contest was the one thing they did to keep everybody happy. After all, if you were promised the chance to win enough magic to make your wildest dreams come true, it would stop you moaning in a hurry. Saga had been sceptical of this, but Afi had just chortled and reminded her that most people *liked* magic.

'Do you think they'll enter?' Saga grinned, gesturing at the children who were setting each other challenges on the other side of the lake, pretending that they were competing in the Fifth Winter.

'You have to eat the most snow to win!' one of the children shrieked, chasing the others with handfuls of snow.

Saga laughed as the smallest child managed to give their older sibling a face full of snow.

'Saga, did you hear me?'

Saga shifted her attention back to her friend. 'What?'

'The Fifth Contest.' Dag shifted on his skates, reluctantly meeting her eyes. 'I think I might enter.'

Saga stared at him. Not too far away, Bjørn lifted his head, sensing her mood change.

'You know I'm rubbish at rune-work,' Dag continued. 'I've got barely any magic running through my veins; winning that horn might be the only chance I get to wield some. Think what you could do with magic like that!'

Saga's gaze rose to where her parents' shield shimmered above them. 'That much magic is too dangerous for one person,' she said fiercely. Bjørn stood up and slowly began padding around the ice. If he could pounce on her bad thoughts, he would, but there were some things from which not even Bjørn could protect her. It always helped when he was close, though.

Dag fell silent.

Guilt bubbled in Saga's stomach. 'Are you really going to enter?' she asked in a smaller voice.

'Not this year,' Dag said, and Saga blew out a sigh of relief. 'But one year, I will.' He spun on the ice to face Saga. 'Not all magic is bad,' he said carefully. 'Your parents used their magic to save your life. To save our whole village.'

'But if my mother was that powerful ...' Saga swallowed. If her mother's magic was strong enough to kill, what if Saga had inherited the same magic?

Like Bjørn, Dag always seemed to know what Saga was thinking. 'You don't know if it was her magic or if she used an ice crystal,' he reminded her.

Saga nodded, not trusting herself to speak. Her parents had met four Fifth Winters ago, when they'd both competed in the contest. Neither of them had won, but her mother had made it to the final challenge where she'd impressed a sorcerer enough to give her one ice crystal. A big lump wedged itself in Saga's throat and she felt as if she was back there, hiding under the table, as that flash of silver light poured out from her parents – the last thing she could remember from that night. She shook her head as if she could shake the memory away.

'You need to remember the good things as well as the bad,' Dag said.

But Saga suddenly didn't want to talk about it any more. 'Race you to the other side!' She pushed off with one skate and flew over the ice so fast she thought she might launch into the sky and soar over clouds and birds until her fingertips grazed against the stars and she'd left her sadness behind.

It was much, much later when Saga tiptoed back into her longhouse.

Her stomach growled louder than a bear, reminding her that dinner had been hours ago.

'You're late.' Her afi sat before the fire, carving a small piece of wood. He didn't look up. Again and again, his chisel flowed over the wood, summoning the true shape of the carving to the surface.

'I'm sorry,' Saga burst out, throwing her arms round him.

He patted her shoulder. 'Now, now, what's all this?' he grunted. Saga sniffed back tears. Her afi pulled away and looked seriously at her before reaching out and rubbing his thumb under her eye. 'Reckon we both could have handled this morning better,' he told her. 'It looks like you got more than my blue eyes – my temper's in there too. Did I ever tell you the story of how I got my axe?'

Saga had heard the story several times before, but stories were like the stars; each time you encountered them, you learned them a little better until they became familiar old friends. She was settling in to listen, happy that all had been forgotten and they were back to normal, when her stomach snarled.

'There's food on the – ah,' her afi said, and Saga twisted round just in time to see the platter of roasted meat vanishing into Bjørn's mouth. 'I think that was your punishment for keeping him from his dinner.' Afi laughed, creaking to his knees and spearing a couple of slices of thick rye bread over the fire. When they were toasted, he handed them to Saga, dripping with golden butter. 'Now, I was a young man when I got the notion to visit the elves' smithy. It was said that they lived deep in the caves, several days' travel south from here, where they worked red-gold into weapons that gleamed like stolen dragon scales.'

Saga devoured her toast, licking butter from her fingers as she listened. Bjørn curled up behind her as Saga settled in for the night. These were her favourite times – when she didn't have to think about magic, the sorcerers, her supposed destiny or anything other than being cosy. She rested back against her bear, lying down on the handwoven rugs that warmed up their swept marl floor. The thick wall hangings gently fluttered as the fire made their little longhouse warm as toast, lulling Saga into a deep, dreamless sleep.

CHAPTER THREE
THE MAGIC SHIELD

Saga awoke to the sound of voices.

'I heard tales of one warrior who used his magical winnings to turn every stone in their village into a precious jewel. Now, they push their boats off from glittering emerald shores. Of course, nobody can forget the rumours of that one village that simply disappeared.'

'Better not mention that in front of Saga,' said another voice gruffly.

Afi, Saga thought.

'Is she still refusing her destiny?' the first voice asked.

'She is deathly afraid of magic. I can't even tell how powerful she may or may not be since she won't carve a single rune,' Afi said. 'I called you here for your assistance. Perhaps you can help persuade her to try. She listens to me about everything but not this.' Afi's sigh made Saga's throat catch. 'She is my starlight,' he admitted. 'She makes my days shine brighter, but if I cannot teach her how to use her magic then I have failed her. And the seers.'

'Do not fear yet,' came the answering voice, who Saga finally placed as the Jarl. 'The seers see all things, past and present. They may live apart from us, but they are wise protectors of the North, and they shared this prophecy with you for a reason. Saga will meet her destiny, of that I am certain.'

Afi sighed again. 'But if I cannot help her –'

'It is the hardest thing to let a child go,' the Jarl interrupted, 'but this destiny is Saga's and you cannot bear it for her.'

Saga stared into the fire at the heart of the longhouse. Bjørn was softly snoring next to her, but Saga was wide awake now. She felt like thunder: all tight and hot and angry, on the verge of a storm. The prophecy was like a sky heavy with snow; it weighed down on her, making it hard to breathe, impossible to escape. How could she have a magical destiny when all she wanted was to curl up by the fire with her bear and listen to stories? She pressed her face against Bjørn's fur and took a few deep breaths, his familiar smoky scent calming her enough to get out of bed. Her afi must have carried her here last night after she'd fallen asleep, her head stuffed with tales of elves and epic journeys. She had a quick wash with the cold water in the bucket nearby, got dressed and tugged a reindeer-antler comb through her knotted silver hair. Even in the dark, her hair gleamed like a polished coin. She'd heard tales that the sorcerers' hair was silver too, marked by strong currents of magic that had charged through them, but Saga didn't remember the magic that had scorched her hair silver, only the moon-bright light that had poured out of her parents as the longhouse tore apart and the trolls howled. Saga set her antler comb down, pausing to glance up at the silver scorch marks on the wooden ceiling. Afi had rebuilt their home, making it stronger and safer than ever, but it was still marked by that day. Like Saga. She shuddered, pulling back the wall hanging and greeting their guest.

'Good morning, Saga,' the Jarl said pleasantly. He and Afi were drinking from horns as they sat and chatted at the table.

Saga nodded and began making the morning porridge. Bjørn's snores were still rumbling through the longhouse, but he'd wake up and nudge his nose into her palm any moment now, demanding breakfast. Dag had a forest cat that would yowl and leap up on to his shoulder any time her food bowl ran low and it always made Saga laugh, imagining if Bjørn acted the same way. She mixed oats and milk, painfully aware of the silence that hung between the Jarl and her afi. Her cheeks burned as she imagined them watching her, wondering if she'd heard their conversation. Well, she had and she didn't like it one bit. She clanged the ladle loudly into the cauldron.

'I hear that you're still having some trouble with the runes,' the Jarl said.

Saga tried not to glare at him. He was the ruler of their village and once had led them to several victories in battle. Before the shield had isolated them, of course. Now, he was as old as Afi, with matching grey hair, neatly combed back, and golden brooches clasping his rune-patterned cloak together. There were so many different runes embroidered on to his cloak that it set Saga's teeth on edge. She dished out the porridge and poured extra honey on to hers, hoping that if she shovelled enough into her mouth she wouldn't have to speak to him about the thing that she was most afraid of.

Afi used his sternest voice: 'Saga.'

'I'm not having trouble with the runes – I just don't use them,' she answered. The Jarl exchanged a significant look with her afi. Saga bristled. 'And I don't see how that's any of your business,' she added hotly.

Afi stood. 'Show some respect when you speak to your elders. The Jarl is here to help oversee your first rune carvings. Now that you are twelve, you can't avoid your destiny any longer. It is time, Saga.'

'No.' Saga stood up so quickly that her chair fell back on to the floor. 'No, you can't make me.' The storm that had been brewing inside her all morning suddenly erupted. 'I will never use magic!' she shouted, and darted to the door, grabbing her furs and little pouch before she ran outside.

'Saga!' her grandfather called after her, but she ignored the hurt in his voice and kept running, her leather boots sinking into the snow. She ran past Dag, who took one look at her face and let her go. He always knew when she needed to be alone. She ran until she had reached the foot of the mountains, where she slowed and began to trudge up and up and higher still. Higher than she'd ever dared before.

A soft padding of paws sounded behind her. Saga turned and buried her face in Bjørn's fur. 'Why can't Afi love me for who I am?' Her teeth chattered as she spoke and Bjørn whined anxiously. 'All right, all right.' Saga pulled on her fur cape and wool-lined mittens, stamping her boots in the snow to warm up her feet. She didn't begrudge his presence; she and Bjørn were two sides of the same moon.

Saga gazed out at her village. It sat below, nestled into the fjords and glowing with a hundred pinpricks of light from its wooden buildings. This far north, winter came with a darkness that grew and grew until it eclipsed the day. Now they would not set eyes on the sun until spring arrived. But Saga didn't mind because with the unending night came the lights in the sky: shimmering curtains that rippled in gemstone colours. They ribboned and twirled through the sky like dancers. Saga looked up. The Northern Lights were glimmering as far as she could see. She didn't understand why the sorcerers would want to distil them for their magic. To her, they were the most beautiful when they ran across the sky, wild and free. Sometimes Dag would squint up at the night sky, claiming to glimpse Bifrost, the bridge that led to another world, but that was much further north. No mortal human could set foot on the bridge, not even a sorcerer, but they still kept an eye on it just in case something happened to peek through from the other side. Nothing like that had happened in hundreds of years, but you could never be too careful.

Saga watched the Northern Lights, wondering what another world might look like.

But they weren't the only thing glimmering in the sky.

Her stomach dropped, heavy as wet fur.

She was close enough to brush up against her parents' shield – and it was whispering with magic.

Saga had spent more than half her life looking up at this near-invisible layer that stretched out between the mountains that surrounded their fjord, forming a roof over their village. Water and snow and sunlight could move through it, but no animal or person – well, almost none.

Only Saga and her afi were granted safe passage through the shield. The magic recognized its kin. Dag liked to moan about this when they hunted or skated together – as if he would be tempted to hike through the mountains or run off on some adventure when, really, Saga knew Dag was happiest curling up in front of the fire with his cat. Despite what he claimed about wanting to enter the contest on the next Fifth Winter, Dag was a lot more similar to Saga than he'd admit.

Besides, the fisherfolk and raiders had their doorway in the shield through which they could sail their longboats away, and Dag could hop onboard if he was desperate for some heroic quest. But everybody else knew that the shield kept them safe from the troll attacks that plagued other villages. They didn't mind staying inside the shield – the mountains were dangerous. Even Saga had never tried to leave before.

'You killed my mother and father,' she said, watching the magic whisper and ripple in front of her, and hating it. It was a constant reminder that she had lost her parents and she didn't want to live under it any more. She wished it would just disappear.

She sucked in a deep, cold breath.

And stepped through.

CHAPTER FOUR
MOUNTAIN TROLLS

The air crackled. Saga squeezed her eyes tightly shut and kept walking, until the shield had stopped tingling against her skin and all she could feel was the deep cold of the North.

When she looked back, the shield was like a thin veil of silvery water behind her. It rippled as a white-tailed eagle brushed its wings against it and Saga shivered. On the other side, Bjørn whined unhappily at her. The sound tugged at her heart. She'd only wanted to step out for a moment, to see what it would be like, but when Bjørn pawed at the shield, trying to reach her, she regretted it. They had never been this far apart before.

The wind bit deeper. Saga was about to step back through the shield when the whispering sound of its magic began echoing around her head. She stood on the frozen mountaintop, listening to its song. It sent her thoughts swirling like a thick mist. Now and then, she saw images. They were hazy and distant, but she knew what they were: runes. And then she felt something else. Something strange.

It took her a moment to realize what it was – her own magic was dancing under the surface of her skin, called to life by the crackling shield next to which she was standing. Saga shook her head as if she could shake it all away.

She was so distracted that she didn't realize Bjørn had started growling until he began snapping his jaws.

Something was crunching over the snow. Something very large and heavy. And then: a lower, guttural snarling.

Saga whirled round. *That wasn't Bjørn.* She slowly backed towards the shield. But, before she reached it, a troll appeared. It had just cleared the mountaintop and she could hear more lumbering footsteps coming her way. Fear gripped her in its icy talons.

The village had heard rumours of troll raids each time the fishing boats returned, but the shield usually kept them safe and Saga hadn't seen one since that terrible day seven years ago.

It was a giant with three heads. Saga stared up at it, frozen in place. It wore layers of wolf pelts and its skin looked like cracked stone. Its grey hair was wild and, here and there, plants had taken root in it. Moss lived in the pockets between its skin flaps. All at once, its six beady eyes swivelled to Saga. It raised the uprooted tree it was carrying like a club and snarled louder.

Its snarl was answered by what sounded like a hundred more. Saga whipped her head around just in time to see more trolls emerging on the mountaintop.

Saga's heart slammed into her ribcage at the terrible sight.

Bjørn whined, pawing frantically at the shield as Saga turned, her arms outstretched, ready to throw herself back through to the other side. Then the tree-club came whistling down through the air, hitting the snow beside her. Though it had missed her, the mountain seemed to shift from the impact, throwing Saga down. She was sweating inside her furs, her fear swelling into panic. Trolls could stir up avalanches that took out entire villages. That's why the god of thunder, Thor, had driven most of them into exile with his thunderbolts long, long ago. But the gods hadn't been seen in hundreds of years and the trolls were no longer in hiding.

Bjørn roared. Saga looked up just in time to see the tree hurtle down towards her again. She didn't have time to move. She was going to be smashed into the snow . . .

But the shield, her parents' last whisper of magic, had been created with their dying wish: to protect their daughter. And so, with a wind-rush that lifted Saga up on to her toes, the entire shield snapped up and wrapped itself round Saga. Her silver hair glowed like moon-beams as she gasped at the force of the magic, fizzing and spitting around her. The shield was no longer protecting the village.

The trolls backed away from her at once. With a stomach-sinking realization, Saga shouted and waved her arms at the trolls, trying to attract their attention to her once more.

But it was too late.

The trolls started lumbering down the mountain, towards the now unshielded village.

And Saga, slowly drifting down on to the snow, was powerless to stop them.

CHAPTER FIVE
ATTACK ON THE VILLAGE

Saga jumped on to Bjørn's back and rode him down the mountain, taking a different route to avoid the trolls. Fast and faster, until the stars blurred overhead and she tasted snow, kicked up by Bjørn's huge paws. Fast enough to overtake the trolls. As they ran and slid down the mountain, the magic shield weakened, melting around Saga like ice until it disappeared completely. Though she hated the magic, had feared it since her parents had died for it, it was their last mark on this realm and now it was gone.

She let out a little choked cry then sat taller on her bear's back.

'Trolls!' she screamed as they entered the village. 'Trolls are coming!'

She rode past the forge, where blades and axes were born in fire so hot it was white as ice. Iron-workers snatched their weapons out of the fires now, holding them high as they ran to where the village met the mountains. She rode past the mead hall, where the Jarl ruled and they feasted on long tables. Someone blew a birch-bark horn to signal danger and the warning spread quickly. People ran from their longhouses, hid their children and bared their axes. Dag was nowhere to be seen. Saga rode through them all towards the most important person in the whole village: her afi. When she saw him standing outside their home, she slid down from Bjørn, her chest aching. 'The mountain trolls are coming,' she told him.

'And the shield?' he asked quietly.

Saga lowered her eyes. 'It was my fault.'

'Saga, listen to me,' her afi said urgently, crossing the ground between them and lifting her up on to Bjørn's back. 'We don't have much time. You must run. Run before the trolls reach us.'

'No.' Saga folded her arms across her fur cape. 'I will stay and fight with you.' Ever since she could walk, her afi had been teaching her how to fight with axe and knife and now she was strong enough to lift a shield high.

In the distance, she heard the mountains shuddering as the trolls trudged down them, felt the earth beneath her bear's paws tremble as they reached the village. In minutes, they'd be here.

'Go to the Far North,' her afi insisted. 'You must tell the sorcerers what is happening in the villages and towns. Only they have the power to defend us from the trolls.'

Saga felt as if he had doused her with ice water. 'I can't. The magic –'

Her afi's glacier-blue eyes burned into hers. '*Víkingr* blood courses through your veins. You are braver than a raider and fiercer than an eagle. Remember your destiny, Saga – the fate of the North rests in your hands.' He lifted a small pouch on to her lap then unstrapped his scabbard and fastened it round her, giving her his knife.

'No,' Saga protested. 'I can't leave you!'

'You must,' he said fiercely. But, though his voice was as strong as the mountains, his eyes betrayed him: Afi was afraid.

Saga shrank back, panicking. If even her afi, a legendary warrior, was scared, then things were even worse than she'd thought.

Afi drew his battleaxe. It was red-gold and bore the single ice crystal that had long lost its magic. 'Go now, Saga.' His voice cracked. 'Leave at once and ride fast for the Far North. You are our last hope.'

Saga's eyes filled. 'Afi,' she whispered.

'I know. Safe travels, my Saga.' He pressed a hand to her cheek. 'Remember, if you can find Odin's wagon in the sky, you will never be lost. The stories of the gods are written in the stars for us to find our way in this world.' Saga desperately held on to his arm, but, as the snarling and thundering footfalls sounded closer, he pulled away, drawing a quick rune that sent the wind rushing towards Bjørn, pushing his paws over the snow, forcing them to leave. 'Now *go*!'

Bjørn took off at a lumbering run and Saga clung on tightly to his fur. They ran through the village and up a mountain on the opposite side – one that the trolls hadn't come from.

'Stop,' Saga whispered, her throat thick. Bjørn slowed and she slipped down his back and stood there in horror, watching the scene that unfolded below. What if her afi – she swallowed the thought. It was too painful to even consider.

The village's fiercest raiders ran towards the trolls, yelling the battle cry 'Tyr!', invoking the god of war. Spears, axes and shields were raised against them. But the trolls were taller and thicker than trees and could not be cut down. Saga spotted her afi entering the battle, wielding his axe like the fiercest of warriors. Moonlight glinted from his axe handle; she would have recognized it anywhere. But her afi wasn't as powerful as her parents had been and didn't stop to use magic. Only a few villagers held that kind of talent and their blades were stronger than their runes, but the trolls' skin was hard like a rock and could not be pierced. These were mountain trolls, creatures of stone with all the ferocity and violence of nature's wild ways.

Saga refused to look away, even as the villagers began to lose. They were brave and she would be too. But the last time the trolls had invaded their village, Saga's parents had defended it. Now Saga was the one who was meant to hold the fate of the North in her hands – perhaps that marked her as the new defender of her village. Sucking in a trembling breath, she bent down and tried to draw the same rune her afi had, to send a gale tumbling down the mountain and over the trolls. But her hand was shaking and fear was clawing at her mind, and she wasn't sure whether or not she'd managed to finish the rune before her stomach turned and she was sick on the snow where she'd tried to carve it. Either way, nothing happened. Just a dull ringing in Saga's ears and a nasty taste in her mouth.

Bjørn whined, lowering his head and shoulders so that she could climb back to the safety of his back.

Now the trolls were circling the villagers, almost as if they were –

'They're rounding them up,' Saga realized.

A troll that was larger than the others slowly stomped

through the streets, dragging a cage behind it. Saga squinted. The cage was white, probably made from animal bones lashed together with twine. She grimaced. At least she *hoped* it was made from animal bones. There were already people inside, shouting and pulling at the giant bars. Saga's stomach clenched when she realized who they were. The hidden children. Some of the trolls must have been hunting them down while the others fought.

'They found Dag,' Saga whispered, spotting his black hair as he tried to get free.

She watched as the rest of the villagers were herded into the giant cage. Afi was one of the last to go, and for a moment Saga thought she saw him stare in her direction and nod, before a troll batted him inside the cage. Saga yelped, launching herself in his direction, desperate to do something, *anything*, but Bjørn yanked her back, his teeth clamped over her furs. With a great tearing sound, the biggest troll ripped two trees out of the frozen earth. Two other trolls dropped the cage on top of the trees and lifted them like they were nothing more than sticks, each troll carrying two ends as they walked away with the cage.

Saga craned her neck to see in which direction they were leaving the village.

The trolls were taking them north.

CHAPTER SIX
LOST IN THE SNOW

The trolls continued north. Saga, who wasn't ready to leave her afi yet, was silently following at a distance. 'It's not like I'm disobeying Afi,' she told Bjørn. 'I need to go this way anyway.' He grunted in reluctant agreement and Saga went quiet again. It had begun to snow and flakes collected in her hood and on her eyelashes. She blinked them away, staring harder at the trolls and the bone cage two of them were carrying. If she squinted, she could just make out her afi's strong back and Dag's spill of black hair at the back of the cage. Were they searching for her? They knew she had escaped the trolls ... She couldn't stop worrying about why the trolls had taken them in the first place. Afi had told her to ask the sorcerers for help, but that would take a long time and what if Afi and Dag were in more serious danger and couldn't wait?

Snow started to fill in the giant footprints.

'We need to hurry, Bjørn,' Saga whispered urgently, sinking her mittens deeper into his fur, 'or we're going to lose them.' But the sky was cloud-thick, hiding the moon and stars, and Saga didn't dare light a torch. Soon, it grew too dark to see where the trolls had gone. Away from her sheltered village, the wind roared its frozen breath over Saga, showering her with snow. Shivering, she tugged her hood tighter round herself and hung on to Bjørn as he battled a path through the wild weather, snuffling and grunting. 'I wish we could see the stars,' Saga whispered to him. 'I don't know if we're still heading north or not. I think –' she swallowed – 'I think we might be lost.' As soon as she said it, she hugged Bjørn tighter. The North was vast and she was just one girl who had been sent on a dangerous journey she'd never wanted. Home felt very far away now.

One of Bjørn's paws suddenly sank into a patch of deep snow.

It unbalanced him and Saga tried to hold on, but her mittens slipped on his back and she toppled off.

'Bjørn!' she shouted. 'Bjørn?' Feeling with her arms out, she stumbled across the snow, searching for him in the darkness. Her mittens touched fur and she sighed in relief. 'There you are.' But –

'I am not your bear, child,' said a voice.

Saga jolted back. One hand fell to her afi's knife. 'Who are you?' She whipped round, trying to see through the night. 'Where's Bjørn?'

'An old friend. Come. Your bear will wait.' With a sudden fizz, a torch roared to life. The person trudged away, holding it. They wore a long, hooded fur cloak and their back was bent over, from age rather than the howling wind, given the way they walked. Saga hesitated. She saw nothing but moon-white snow illuminated in the pool of firelight. Where had the trolls gone? And where was Bjørn?

'Come,' the person repeated. 'You will not be able to help anyone if the snow swallows you whole.'

Saga wasn't sure she trusted this person, but she was even more scared of being alone, lost in the dark and snow. She slowly followed the figure. Still, she kept a hand on the hilt of her knife.

After a short distance, a mountain reared in front of them. The stranger raised their torch and in the sputtering light, Saga made out a dark hollow staining the side of the mountain: a cave. She glanced back, searching for Bjørn, worry churning her stomach like an ice storm, until she was suddenly cast into darkness.

Saga scurried after the torchlight, following the stranger's path, carving through the snow, wending between thin trees and up to where the mountain yawned open. Saga took a deep breath and stepped into the cave.

Fire flickered over the rune-carved walls. Little bunches of dried herbs and feathers were hung above them and a crooked staff leaned against the entrance, thrumming with magic.

Saga had walked into a witch's cave.

CHAPTER SEVEN
THE WITCH'S CAVE

'You're a witch,' Saga said nervously.

'Yes. A seer.' The stranger shed their cloak, shrinking down into the figure of an elderly woman with clouded eyes. She was wearing the colourful dress and cat-fur hat of the witches and looked as ancient as the Yggdrasill tree that held the worlds together – and more powerful than Saga could imagine.

Witches were creatures of the night, their bones soaked in moonlight. Some witches held spells on the tips of their tongues, others listened in to the winds and tides, but only a few were like this one, peering through the fabric of time to see what was yet to come.

Saga shivered at the thought. 'What do you want with me?' she asked aloud.

'Saga Thorolfsdottir,' the seer mused. 'It has been some time since our paths first crossed. I have been awaiting your arrival ever since.' She gestured at the fire pit smoking in the entrance of the cave and the thick logs that framed it. 'Be seated.'

Saga obeyed, tugging off her wool-lined mittens with her teeth and warming her hands on the fire. It was always a good idea to listen to a seer. They were wise protectors of the North, who knew everything. The valley below was dark and she could spot nothing moving through it. No trolls, no bone cage and no bear. Her heart sank deeper in her chest, sore and heavy. She blinked her eyes fiercely and turned her attention to the seer. 'I don't remember meeting you before.' Her voice was hesitant, for she had been told a story, one that she had tried to unhear – the one that made her afi's voice glow with pride even as his forehead creased with worry. She watched the old woman carefully.

The seer busied herself with ladling out something from a cauldron bubbling over the fire. She passed a small wooden bowl to Saga. 'Eat.'

Saga slurped the soup down. She was cold and hungry and if the seer had wanted to wish her harm she would have left her outside. Besides, everybody knew that witches looked after the North. Maybe – she eyed the seer hopefully – she would help Saga save her afi and Dag so that she didn't need to journey all the way to the Far North, where the sorcerers lived. Though she needed to find Bjørn first. It was unlike her bear to leave her; it felt as if she had misplaced her heart.

The seer's joints creaked as she sat on the opposite log. Her sigh sounded like the wind blowing through trees. 'That is a quest you shall have to take alone.'

Saga started. 'Can you –'

'No, I cannot read your mind,' the seer interrupted. 'Your thoughts are plain for all to see.'

Saga put her bowl down. 'What quest?' she asked quietly.

'Why, the one to save your village, of course.'

Panic washed over Saga like the tide. 'My afi told me to travel to the Far North. To where the sorcerers live in their ice castle and rule over the tundra. He said that only the sorcerers could save them now.' She still worried that she was leaving her afi in danger, but she trusted him more than she trusted the moon not to fall from the sky and if he had told her to travel to the Far North, then to the Far North she would travel.

'Hmm.' The seer stared into the fire. Her white eyes reflected the embers that danced like tiny stars. 'He sounds like a wise man. Perhaps you should heed his words.'

Saga eyed her suspiciously. 'It was a seer that visited my afi when I was a baby and told him that I had a magical destiny. Was that you?'

The seer said nothing.

Saga rubbed her forehead. It was late and she couldn't stop thinking about the cosy little longhouse she shared with her afi, wishing that she had never run from him. If she had only stayed, none of this would have happened. They would have been whiling away the evening with King's Table, her favourite of the games Afi carved to sell to the village, the longhouse warm with firelight, Bjørn slumbering at their feet. Afi chortling when Bjørn let out a particularly loud snore. Her heart ached to think of him in that cage.

'Can you tell me anything else? What am I supposed to do when I get there? How do I enter the sorcerers' castle to ask them for help? And how can I save my village when I'm too scared to –' The words *use the runes* caught in her throat and she choked to a stop.

'Love is greater than fear, child.' The seer poured a second bowl of soup and passed it over to Saga. 'When the time comes, you will make the right decision.'

Saga accepted the bowl glumly. 'Why did you bring me to your cave?' Time was trickling through her fingers like a fistful of water.

The seer leaned closer. 'What kind of quest would it be if the hero froze to her death in a snowstorm the moment she stepped outside her village?' Was it Saga's imagination or did the seer's eyes shine a little brighter? Her mouth tip up at one corner? 'If you remember one thing from tonight, let it be this: the bravest hero does not tread her path alone.' She lifted her face to the sky. 'The storm has shifted. It is time for you to start your journey.' She rose to her feet like a tree unfolding her branches. 'The contest shall start soon.'

'The contest?' Saga frowned. 'Wait, are you talking about the Fifth Winter?' In all the chaos of the troll attack, she'd forgotten that she wouldn't be the only one journeying to the Far North. 'But I'm not going to enter that – I'm only going to ask the sorcerers for help,' Saga said.

The seer gave her a peculiar look.

'Are you saying I *should* enter?' Saga's frown deepened. 'I don't have the kind of magic for that. I don't know why your prophecy thinks I do,' she added a little sulkily.

'A hornful of ice crystals would solve your troll problem faster than a cat after a squirrel,' the seer replied, ushering her out of the cave.

'I suppose I could pretend to enter the contest just to get into the castle?' Saga turned to the seer, but shock pinned her in place. The mountainside was smooth. No cave marred its snowy slope. Both the cave and the seer had vanished as if they were never there.

Her breath came faster, feathering out as she pulled on her mittens and touched the mountain. Nothing. She snapped her hand back, realizing she was alone in the dark. She'd never been away from the lanterns and fires of her village before, never had to tread a path without her trusty bear at her side. But Bjørn was lost too, and she had to be strong for him. Steeling herself, she took step after careful step, trying not to panic as she walked down into the valley.

With a sudden huff of hot air, Bjørn came lumbering out of the trees and into her open arms.

'Bjørn!' Saga hugged him. 'I've been so worried about you.'

Bjørn bumped his head against her shoulder with a soft whine. Saga hugged him harder. 'I'm never letting you out of my sight again,' she said fiercely. She put one hand on his back and they walked together through the valley. Now that the storm had calmed, the valley was blanketed in fresh snow, covering any tracks the trolls and villagers might have left. But the wind had blown the clouds away and, above, a dazzling display of stars twinkled at them.

Saga stopped and searched the skies. 'There's Odin's wagon.' She pointed out a constellation to her bear, remembering all the times that Afi had shown it to her. His gruff voice filled her memories as if he was standing next to her: 'If you can find Odin's wagon in the sky, you will never be lost. The stories of the gods are written in the stars for us to find our way in this world.'

Saga clambered on to Bjørn's back and together they followed the stars further north.

CHAPTER EIGHT
A WHITE REINDEER

That night, Saga dreamed about runes.

She wasn't carving them into stone or wood, but drawing them with her finger in the air. They left curving shapes behind that she didn't recognize; these were not any runes that she'd seen Afi make. Bubbling with magic, they glowed the bright blue of ancient ice before turning into her afi's fierce blue eyes. His mouth moved, but she couldn't work out what he was saying and then she began to fall, sliding down the deck of a boat, slipping through her afi's arms as he reached out to catch her and down, down, down ... She woke with a gasp when she hit snow.

Bjørn patted her with his paw.

'I'm awake, I'm awake,' Saga grumbled, getting to her feet and brushing the powder from her furs. Stifling a yawn, she jerked her head towards the trees. 'Come on, let's make camp.'

With the trees sheltering them, Saga collected dry firewood before digging inside the small pouch her afi had given her. One of the things inside was a firestarter: a strip of mushroom beaten, charred and boiled in urine until it could smoulder for days. Saga gently blew on it and it flamed. Soon, they had a roaring fire. She huddled up against Bjørn as they shared some salted fish Afi had also packed. As Bjørn slurped up the snow Saga melted for water, she thought over what the seer had told her.

'I don't know if the trolls are still heading further north or not but I think we need to,' she said to Bjørn as she set down her drinking cup. The bear immediately got his nose stuck in it. Saga tickled his belly. 'It's just the two of us now,' she told him. He shook off her cup and looked up at her seriously. 'And I think we're going to have to pretend to enter the contest just to get inside the sorcerers' castle.' A soft growl rumbled in Bjørn's chest. Saga nestled closer to him. 'It will be all right. I'm not going to actually enter the contest. Once the sorcerers have agreed to help, we can leave straight away and go and get Afi and Dag and everyone, and go back home, where we all belong.'

Outside their little fire, the world was vaster, darker and lonelier than Saga had imagined. And every time she worried about what the trolls were going to do to her afi, Saga felt smaller. She sighed and rubbed her head, trying to remember the stories Afi had told her of the contest and the time her parents had entered it. But all the stories had been about how Saga's father had fallen so in love with her mother that when he lost the first challenge and had to leave the castle he waited outside in the snow for days, until her mother failed at the last challenge and joined him. Then there were the stories about that village that had disappeared after a winner went home with a horn full of ice crystals. Saga stared at the fire. Magic was dangerous, but what if it was the only way to save Dag and Afi? The thought of something happening to either one of them was even scarier than magic. Bjørn whined, but she gritted her teeth and reached out a hand.

'I *have* to try. What if I could save them?'

Using her finger like a knife, she started carving the rune she'd seen in her dream. Her hand trembled. Sweat dribbled down the back of her furs and her breathing fogged into the air. Still, she tried until her vision swirled and she felt so dizzy she was nearly sick. Bjørn huffed, pawing at her until she abandoned the rune.

'I can't do it,' she whispered miserably, leaning against his soft flank.

Suddenly, the trees nearest to Saga began to tremble and shake. She stood up, laying a hand on Bjørn as he tensed, sensing whatever was lurking there.

The ground shook.

Saga looked to the stars; thunder was the rumble of Thor's wagon, rolling across the sky – but the stars hadn't shifted. She began packing her little pouch in a hurry. This far north, she wouldn't survive without it.

Then there were footsteps. Massive, tree-rattling footsteps, coming their way. Saga was desperately reaching for the last bit of fish when a troll stepped out of the trees. Though this one had only one head, its eyes were hungry.

Saga dropped the fish. Bjørn reared on to his back legs, puffing himself up, ready to fight the troll.

'Bjørn, no!' she yelled.

But Bjørn was a fiercely protective bear. He roared. And the troll unhinged its jaw and roared back. Its breath blew Saga's hood down, hot and rancid against her face. She gagged at the stench, her ears ringing as she tugged at Bjørn's fur.

'Come on, we have to go,' she cried.

Bjørn tipped forward, landing on all four paws. Saga clambered on to his back and he broke into a run, heading away from the warmth of the fire and back into the night.

But the troll wasn't finished with them yet. It bellowed and gave chase.

Bjørn gathered speed, his paws padding in the snow like snowshoes as they fled northwards over the land.

Each time Saga looked back, the troll seemed to be closer. 'It's catching up with us,' she shouted, wiping her eyes and nose as they watered from rushing through the frozen night. The next time she looked, it was close enough to spot the shrubs nesting in its hairy ears. The time after that, she could see the stones that encrusted its knuckles as it reached out to swipe at them.

Saga ducked and grabbed for her knife.

A bellow sounded in the distance. The troll paused, listening. Bjørn managed to carve out some distance between them, but Saga didn't dare sheath her knife just yet. Then the troll turned and darted back, disappearing into the dark. Saga knew that without lighting a torch she wouldn't know if any others might be lurking, just out of sight.

'Well done, Bjørn.' She patted her bear, suddenly exhausted, having been awake the entire night. Judging by the deep blue tint creeping up the horizon, it was now late morning. Though the sun never rose above the mountains in winter, each day granted them a few hours of rich blue light that set the fjords aglow. It did mean Saga had lost the stars, but if they continued their current path, inland from the fjords, eventually they would reach the end of their world. The sorcerers lived beyond that point, on islands made entirely of ice, where white bears hunted and prowled, and horned whales clashed in the sea.

Bjørn eventually slowed to a comfortable pace and Saga settled down for a long day of riding her bear. They passed endless white landscapes, Saga drifting off to sleep. Until – She jerked upright. 'Did you see that? I could have sworn that something just moved.' She rubbed her eyes to see better. 'Please don't let it be another troll . . .'

Out of the snow stepped a white reindeer.

Saga squeezed her legs round Bjørn and he came to a quiet stop.

The reindeer walked towards Saga and her bear and halted nervously. Then Saga spotted the harness wrapped round its midsection; it was pulling a sled. And on the sled was a girl who looked the same age as Saga.

'Hello,' Saga said, feeling more than a little foolish.

The girl replied in one of the Sámi languages. Her eyes and hair were the earthy brown of the forest in early autumn and her pale skin was reddened from the wind and cold. Saga didn't speak Sámi. But Bjørn seemed fascinated with the girl. He ambled over to her sled and Saga was about to call him back in case the girl was afraid, when to her amazement, Bjørn rested his head on the sled, allowing the girl to stroke him behind his ears.

'He is beautiful,' the girl told Saga, switching to Norse. 'How did he come to be yours?'

'He isn't mine,' Saga said a little defensively. 'We belong to each other.'

Afi had told her that one day, when he'd been chopping firewood outside their longhouse, he'd returned to discover Saga cuddled up with a lost brown bear cub. Nobody had seen Bjørn wander through their village. Even her parents, who had been inside the longhouse, eating and talking, had sworn that the door had not opened. When she grew old enough to understand the stories that her afi wove, Saga suspected that Bjørn was her *fylgja*, a guardian spirit that mirrored her *hugr*, her immortal character. A *fylgja* was usually hidden inside a person, like warriors that held the wolf as their totem or like Dag, who pretended that the eagle was his when it was secretly a deer. But Saga was lucky enough to wear her guardian spirit outside of her person, treading through life with her best bear friend forever at her side.

'I understand,' said the girl in such a way that Saga felt that she did. 'Where are you travelling to?'

'To the Far North,' Saga told her.

The girl gave her an evaluating look. 'For the contest?'

After a brief hesitation, Saga nodded. This girl was a stranger and didn't need to know that Saga was only pretending to enter the Fifth Winter to get inside the castle. Besides the seer, she was the first person Saga could remember meeting outside the safety of her village, but if Bjørn trusted her then Saga knew she could too.

'As am I. Perhaps we should travel together. Your bear is tiring.'

Saga's stomach pinched with guilt. 'I know,' she said quietly. She had asked too much from him already and they still had a long way to go. 'I would be grateful to ride in your sled with you.'

The girl moved over and Saga slid down Bjørn's back and sat next to her.

'I am Ruvsá,' said the girl, pulling her blankets over them both. They were made of thick, fuzzy wool and very warm.

'Saga.'

Ruvsá gave the reindeer a command and they began to move. Bjørn ambled along at their side. 'I come from a family of reindeer farmers,' Ruvsá told Saga. 'But this winter has been hard – and winning the contest would help.'

Saga watched Ruvsá guide her reindeer without saying anything. Saga knew villagers who had sailed a little way up the coast to trade with the Sámi so she knew that Ruvsá's reindeer-fur coat and hooded cape were called a *beaska* and a *luhkka*, and that reindeer herders loved and respected their animals. She also knew it was rude to ask how many reindeer were in a herd. Instead, she asked, 'What's your reindeer's name?'

Ruvsá's smile warmed the night. 'Snowflake.' She glanced at Saga. 'So why do you want to win the magic?'

Saga chewed her lip. She wasn't sure how much to tell Ruvsá, though it could be useful to learn more about the contest just in case – her village had been hidden under a shield for many years, robbing them of visitors from the outside world, like storytellers who might have spun tales of what had happened in the last few Fifth Winters. So she sighed and turned to the other girl, telling her, 'My village was attacked by trolls yesterday.'

Ruvsá gasped. 'I am sorry to hear that. Trolls rarely attack the Sámi, but we have heard of the raids on villages all over the North.' Most of the Sámi were nomadic, following their reindeer herds as they moved throughout the year, taking their homes, their *lávvus*, with them. This made them difficult prey for the trolls. Ruvsá went on: 'This past year there were more than usual.'

Saga grimaced. 'I didn't know that. Our village has been protected until now.' She gave no explanation for this but Ruvsá didn't ask for one either and Saga liked her better for it.

The two girls fell into an easy silence and Saga rested her head against the curved back of the sled, watching the blue-stained sky darken, revealing the first stars. Now the day looked like night again. She couldn't help imagining her parents travelling to the Far North all those winters ago, wondering if she was treading the same path now. Yawning, she let her eyes close, and fell into a deep sleep, helped along by the comforting motion of the sled as it gently creaked over the snow.

CHAPTER NINE
WHERE THE SKY MEETS THE SEA

Saga was drawing a rune in the air. Another shape she did not recognize, but dream-Saga seemed to know well, watching as it shimmered and glowed. The seer's voice echoed through her dream: *The contest shall start soon.* Louder and louder until it reverberated through her bones and Saga woke with a start.

The sled had stopped.

Bjørn, Ruvsá and the white reindeer were nowhere to be seen. A flaming torch had been stuck into the snow and Saga scrambled off the sled and looked around.

Ruvsá returned with her arms heaped with fire-wood. 'Ah, you're awake.' Snowflake and Bjørn walked obediently either side of her, much to Saga's surprise.

She had never seen her bear be this affectionate to anyone else before.

'How long did I sleep?' Saga kneeled beside Ruvsá, helping her with the fire.

'All day. It is night now.' Ruvsá brushed her hands on her cloak as the first flames danced over the wood.

Travelling by sled meant that Ruvsá had more supplies than Saga, and she kindly shared her stew, heating it in a pot over the fire as Saga tore her bread in half.

'What do you know about the contest?' Saga asked, dipping her bread into the stew to soften it.

'Not much,' Ruvsá admitted. 'I know that we will be asked to compete in a series of challenges –'

'How many challenges are there?' Saga interrupted. 'Is it still three? Do you know what they'll ask you – I mean, us – to do?' She was curious to see how far Ruvsá would go. She seemed quiet, but Saga felt there was a deep strength inside her that wanted to be let out. Bjørn made a little snuffling noise that sounded like a laugh. Saga eyed her bear, wondering what Bjørn sensed that she could not.

'I think so. My older brother said it was five or six, and that you had to fight white bears with your bare hands for one of them, but that's all probably just his idea of a joke.'

'Why isn't your brother entering the contest too?' Saga scooped the last of her stew up with her fingers, sucking them clean after. The contest sounded impossible, whether Ruvsá's brother was joking or not, and she was glad she wasn't actually entering it. The challenge that had sent her mother home had been to find and ride a winged horse – nobody knew if any winged horses even existed any more. They were incredibly rare and most had died out, but in Afi's stories they were wild and vicious and impossible to get near, let alone ride.

Ruvsá snorted. 'He entered the last one and still hasn't stopped talking about it. If he tried for this one too, his head would grow so big I might have to push him in the sea.'

Saga grinned at her.

'Now come on – our own adventure is calling us.'

They dashed through the night on the sled, exchanging stories of their homes, their friends and family, until they fell asleep. The next morning, Saga spotted water ahead.

And there, at the point where the sky met the sea, roaring and thrashing like a monstrous creature from the deep, their path ended.

The two girls, their bear and reindeer stood at the precipice and stared ahead.

'Are you sure we have to cross that?' Saga asked.

There was no land in sight. Nothing but rough water to the horizon.

'They say that getting to the ice cliffs is the first challenge,' Ruvsá said, but her voice dipped with uncertainty.

Saga closed her eyes for a beat. This was an impossible task – one for which she didn't have time. What was to stop the trolls from devouring Afi and Dag whole and gobbling up their bones before she got back in time to save them? If she could even work out where they were being taken, that is. And she still hadn't carved a single rune. So much for her magical destiny. She hoped the sorcerers would help quickly.

Saga sneaked a look at Ruvsá standing beside her. Her spine straight, her chin lifted to the skies, this was a girl that faced her fears head on. There would probably be a hundred like her fighting to win. A hundred untold stories. Then Saga remembered something else: only the first fifty to enter the Fifth Winter were allowed inside the castle. Her stomach churned. Pretending to enter the contest was her best plan for getting near enough to the sorcerers to ask for their help. It was her *only* plan. And if she couldn't get in –

Bjørn nudged her, giving her his strictest growl.

'Fine, I'll stop worrying,' Saga murmured to him. 'It's not like I can do anything now to change things.'

Saga sighed and scanned the shore beneath them. Something was moving across the ice-coated rocks. She pointed a mitten at it. 'What's that?'

'Probably a seal,' Ruvsá said, but she looked anyway.

'No, it's a person.' Saga's excitement seeped through her, warmer than her afi's best porridge. 'And they've got a boat.'

CHAPTER TEN
CANUTE

Saga slipped and scrambled over the icy rocks, calling out to the person before they could climb into their boat and push off.

Bjørn wandered behind her, traversing the slick shoreline easily.

'Wait!' Saga puffed as she drew up to a boy, who started and turned towards her with eyes as dark grey as the roiling sea. Then his gaze fixed on something behind her, and his fair skin paled to the colour of snow. 'Do *not* move,' he whispered urgently. 'There's a bear behind you!'

Saga couldn't help smiling. 'Don't worry – Bjørn's harmless.'

The boy gaped at her.

'I'm Saga,' she added, 'and that's Ruvsá.' She pointed back to where Ruvsá stood watching them, patting Snowflake. 'Are you headed to the Far North too?' she asked.

The wind tossed his hood back, revealing a splash of chin-length butter-coloured hair. He tugged it back up with a grimace. 'I am.'

'We need a boat to cross the sea.' Saga eyed his small pouch, his pinched expression, evaluating what he might want or need in return. 'We have food we could share if you let us sail to the islands with you?'

The boy looked back out to sea. Saga bit down on her tongue, trying not to let her hope bubble to the surface. After a painstakingly long hesitation, he nodded his head. 'I suppose I could take pity on you and let you come aboard.'

Saga tried not to glower at him, disliking him immediately. She gestured to Ruvsá, letting her know that they had passage.

'I'm Canute,' the boy added. 'I come from Arne, the biggest settlement in the North.' He puffed his chest out proudly. 'You should know, we *always* win the Fifth Winter contest – our warriors are known for being the bravest and fiercest.'

'Uh huh.' Saga crossed her arms, wishing Ruvsá would hurry up saying goodbye to Snowflake. Bjørn growled quietly and Canute's eyes widened. Saga suppressed a smirk. 'Good thing you're all so fearless,' she said instead. 'Bears can smell fear, you know.'

'They can?' Canute stepped back.

'Oh yes,' Saga continued. 'If you were afraid right now, Bjørn would just *leap* –' Reading her mind, Bjørn did a little bunny hop towards Canute, who shrieked and slipped on the ice. Ruvsá joined them then, putting a stop to Saga's teasing. 'I sent Snowflake back home,' Ruvsá said, watching her white reindeer trot away with the sled. 'He'll be happier there and we can't take the sled on the boat anyway.' Snowflake soon melted out of sight in the snow, leaving them free to voyage onwards.

It wasn't until the three children and one big brown bear had piled into the boat that Saga realized that something was wrong with Canute. While she and Ruvsá had taken a pair of oars each, he gripped on to the side of the boat and refused to open his eyes. And, even as the wind threw ice in their faces like a thousand tiny knives, he was sweating. In fact, he looked like Saga felt when she'd tried to draw that rune.

'You're afraid of the sea,' she realized.

Canute gulped. 'Yes,' he admitted in a small voice.

Ruvsá threw a puzzled look at Saga. 'But you have your own boat.'

Canute's voice shrank even smaller and Saga had to crane her head to hear him above the shrieking of the seabirds. 'My mother and my father are both legendary raiders.' His eyes suddenly snapped open, filling with determination. 'That's why I need to win this magic, so I won't be afraid any more. So that I can be what they want me to be.'

Saga's heart gave a painful thump. She knew that feeling well. 'Who do you want to be?' she asked.

A dreamy look settled over Canute's face. 'I want to be a craftsman.' He tapped the bronze brooch that pinned his cloak together, decorated with a great dragon in swirling lines.

'That's beautiful,' Ruvsá said, making Canute beam. Then the boat lurched over a particularly choppy wave and he remembered they were at sea and turned green once again.

Though she'd teased him with Bjørn earlier, Saga would never tease someone about a real fear. Besides, she'd noticed something else. There was a dragon carved into the small figurehead at the front of the boat. And another embroidered on each of his boots.

'Why dragons?' she asked. She tried to hide the suspicion in her voice; for a boy who claimed he wanted to be a craftsman, dragons were a fierce totem. Saga wasn't sure she trusted him yet. And, judging by the way Bjørn kept his distance, he wasn't either.

Canute shrugged. 'My mother's longboat has a dragon figurehead. They are strong and brave like her. Like I wish I was. At sea, of course,' he added quickly. 'On land I'm as fearsome as any warrior.'

'Of course,' Ruvsá muttered under her breath.

Saga's little tickle of suspicion swelled into a storm. If Canute could face his fears to sail to the Far North, he did not need that magic for the courage to sail elsewhere. Which meant he wanted it for something else. But what? She suspected that this boy was like an iceberg – mostly hidden beneath the surface.

A large wave hit the boat, dousing them all in water so cold it made Saga gasp. Bjørn grumbled and Canute yelped, 'Oh no.'

Saga looked ahead: waves were stacked to the horizon, night-black, tipped with only the faintest moon-glow to light their way. They were in deep seas now. She clenched her oars, concentrating on rowing in rhythm with Ruvsá, who sat at the front of the boat with Canute. Bjørn was in the middle to balance the weight and Saga held the rear.

But the water was fierce and their little boat struggled to battle through it. The wind whipped over the sea, and ice began to hurtle down from above: they'd sailed into a polar storm.

In the darkness, Saga tried to ignore the ache building in her muscles, the tiredness that settled in her bones, the cold that stole under her furs like a thief. But the waves were growing and the puddle of water in the bottom of the boat was rising higher and higher.

'We're carrying too much weight,' she shouted over the roaring sea, which seemed hungry to gobble them down into its watery depths.

'Why did you have to bring that bear?' Canute shouted back at her, glaring at Bjørn.

Bjørn growled, a deep rumbling that reverberated through Saga as she struggled with her oars, pressed against her bear. 'Maybe if you were rowing too,' Saga puffed, 'then this wouldn't be so difficult!'

'It's my boat you're about to sink!'

'I'm not sinking it; this storm is sinking it!' As soon as she'd screamed it, Saga fell silent. *They were sinking.* Now she'd never be able to save Afi and Dag. And she and Bjørn would drown. When she glanced at Canute, she saw that his eyes were wet with more than the ice raining down on them.

Saga breathed deeply and pulled one mitten off, thinking of her dream-runes. Facing her fears had to be better than drowning.

But Ruvsá suddenly stood up.

'What are you doing?' Saga asked. Ruvsá didn't seem to hear. Her face was frozen in concentration as she whispered words that Saga couldn't understand. And then she began to sing.

Something clattered against the side of the boat.

Canute yelped and Bjørn growled again, but Ruvsá only sang louder, offering her voice up to the skies in a hauntingly beautiful joik.

Then something scraped against the bottom of the boat and Saga almost dropped her oars.

'What is that?' Canute yelled.

Ruvsá looked down at him, smiling as she sang. With a stomach-sloshing swoop, something pushed their boat up, above the waves. Saga rushed to look over the side of the boat, and then laughed, giddy, as she spotted the pod of humpback whales that had lifted the boat on their backs.

'Ruvsá, you're amazing,' she whooped as the whales started to carry them further north. 'How did you do that?'

Travelling by whale, they soon left the Polar storm far in their wake. As they crossed the sea, the waters grew shallower and were flecked with ice. Above them, the Northern Lights shimmered in iridescent greens and pinks, and stars filled the sky, shaped into more stories than Saga could hold in her head. She wondered if Afi and Dag were looking up at the same stars and wished she could tell them how close she was to sending them help now.

When the whales slowed and the boat nudged against thick pack ice, Saga stood up and stepped on to the frozen sea. 'We're here.'

PART TWO
THE EDGE OF THE WORLD

Saga was a girl afraid of runes, who had walked into the beating heart of magic itself.

CHAPTER ELEVEN
THE SORCERERS' MOUNTAIN

The walk over the pack ice froze Saga's bones. Bjørn's fur was so frosted that he looked like one of the white bears that stalked these islands. The three children dragged Canute's boat over the ice in the howling storm. They kept walking until they couldn't see water, until the world was one of snow and darkness, held firmly in winter's grip.

'We need to leave my boat somewhere safe,' Canute shouted over the vicious wind.

They halted. Saga squinted through the swirling snow. 'I think there's a cave over there.'

There was a cave. When Saga forged ahead, she half expected to see the old seer again, but this was no witch's cave. It was dank and just big enough to pull Canute's boat inside before they continued on their way.

'Does anyone know where the sorcerers' castle is?' Saga's question was muffled, her hood pulled low, fur collar high, leaving only her eyes visible. She was getting worried about how many contestants might have already entered. If the castle only let the first fifty in and there were already fifty there, how would she be able to get inside to ask the sorcerers for help?

'It's north,' Canute said confidently. 'I was taught how to navigate before I could walk. Just follow me.'

'This whole island is north.' Saga's teeth clattered together. 'And huge. We can't spend much longer outside – we'll freeze.'

Ruvsá suddenly stopped. Saga turned to her, waiting for her to speak, but the wind chose that moment to gust harder. It was as if Thor had swept his legendary hammer, Mjölnir, over the sky. The clouds were blown out of sight, revealing a glittering expanse of stars and the moon, sitting heavy in the sky, shining down on a huge mountain. There were meant to be mountains all over these islands, colossal ranges that curved across the land like dragon spines, but this mountain stood alone.

'There it is,' Saga whispered. Her stomach churned like the seas. The mountain had sheer ice sides that were impossible to climb and, high above, an enormous castle made of ice perched on a frozen plateau. It had more towers than Saga could count, with pointed roofs and large windows that glowed an eerie blue. Its spire pierced the sky. Behind it, the mountain clawed up even higher, reaching a twisted peak.

The three children and one bear walked towards it in silence. The closer they got, the smaller Saga felt.

At the foot of the mountain, a large iron door was set into the ice. It was frozen and bore no handle, but it glowed with runes.

Saga's stomach twisted as the magic hummed, high-pitched and shrill. 'Can you hear that?' she asked through gritted teeth.

Ruvsá cast her a curious glance. 'Hear what?'

Saga shook her head. 'It doesn't matter. How do we get inside?'

Canute drew himself up, throwing back his hood. 'I am Canute Gunvaldson and I am here to pledge myself as a contestant for the Fifth Winter contest,' he grandly told the door. 'These are my travelling companions,' he added, gesturing at Saga and Ruvsá.

Saga glared at him. 'Travelling companions?' The runes hummed louder and she winced, hoping that they weren't too late, that the door didn't sense she was only pretending to enter the contest. But, to her astonishment, the great door began to rise. With a deep clunking sound that resonated deep inside the mountain, it rose into the ice, until there was a space large enough for the four of them to enter.

'You can't argue with success,' Canute said, grinning smugly at Saga.

Saga rolled her eyes. Then she took a deep breath, the air so cold it hurt, and walked inside the mountain.

CHAPTER TWELVE
THE RAVEN'S TEST

They stood in a dark ice passage. Lanterns had been mounted on the frozen walls, each one powered by an ice crystal that sent the blue-green glow of the Northern Lights flickering through the passage. Magic. It vibrated through the mountain.

'Come on,' Saga said quietly, leading the way. Her boots crunched on the ice and, beside her, Bjørn's fur was raised. Nerves tingled down her spine, but she ignored them, focusing on the mist she breathed out instead, like a dragon. She sidled a glance at Canute, but his expression gave nothing away. He wasn't boasting about anything so maybe that meant he was nervous.

At Saga's other side, Ruvsá offered her a smile, wide and carefree. 'We did it,' she said. 'We're three of the fifty contestants!'

Saga smiled back, relieved she'd made it inside the castle. Though she couldn't shake the feeling that it had been a little *too* easy.

At the end of the passage, a large iron shield was embedded in the ice. It had a seam running down the middle, suggesting it was another door. 'There must be a way to open it without magic,' Canute said, searching for a handle. 'There aren't any runes on it.'

But Saga and Ruvsá were looking at the huge carved raven that was perched on the shield. It had ice crystals for eyes and seemed to be watching them. Bjørn growled and Saga rested a hand on his back.

'It must be a test of strength.' Canute tried – and failed – to push the doors open. The raven's eyes suddenly flared bright blue and its wings spread across the shield. Canute yelped and stumbled back.

The raven spoke in a deep voice that gave Saga chills. 'Only those who are worthy may pass.'

'How do you decide who's worthy?' she asked.

'Those who are worthy of entrance must have honour and courage. Tell me your greatest secret and you shall pass.'

Ruvsá exchanged a nervous look with Saga.

'Why does telling you our biggest secrets prove that we have honour and courage?' Canute spluttered indignantly.

But the raven only stared back at him.

Saga almost pounced towards the raven, keenly aware of how close the sorcerers were now and how much time had passed since she'd set off for the Far North. She stood on her tiptoes to whisper as quietly as she could, 'I'm afraid of magic.' The raven returned her unblinking look. She waited but ... nothing. Disappointment whirled in like a storm.

Ruvsá stepped forward. 'Let me try,' she said, and Saga switched places with her, annoyed that Canute looked smug again. Saga couldn't hear what Ruvsá had murmured under her breath, but suddenly the raven's wings moved.

'Did you see that?' Saga gasped.

The raven flapped its wings, and the shield doors whooshed open. Ruvsá walked through. 'You have to tell it your deepest secret!' she called back. Canute ran towards the doors, but they slammed shut the second Ruvsá was clear of them. The clang echoed through the corridor, sending icicles plummeting. Saga and Canute ducked before one speared them, hearing them smash into the ice at their feet. Bjørn, who had clamped his paws over his face, huffed worriedly and stood closer to Saga.

'Only those who are worthy may pass,' the raven repeated, sounding even colder.

Saga shivered. She and Canute looked at each other. He crossed his arms and looked down at the ice. 'You might hear me,' he said sullenly.

'Fine,' Saga snapped. Approaching the raven again, she lowered her voice to the tiniest whisper she could manage, determined not to let Canute hear. 'I'm scared of magic, but I keep dreaming about runes,' she told it. The raven refused to budge. 'I have a magical destiny,' she tried instead, getting impatient. Nothing again. 'I'm not *really* going to enter the contest – I just need to get inside the castle?' Still nothing.

'It has to be your *deepest* secret or it won't work,' Canute called.

She turned to glare at him. 'I know that. I'm trying!'

'Let me have a turn, then.' Canute marched over, his breath feathering in the air. 'It's too cold to stand about waiting.'

Saga stood aside. When Canute glanced warily at her, she sighed and moved further back, trying not to let him see how cold she was too. She secretly wiggled her fingers and toes before she became an icicle herself. Bjørn pushed his nose into her arms and she fussed over him, hoping all his fur was keeping him warm.

Annoyingly, the shield doors flew open for Canute. 'Have fun.' Canute smirked as he strutted through, ignoring Saga's scowl and leaving her and her bear alone with the raven.

She took a deep breath. 'It was my fault my parents' shield vanished and the trolls attacked my village?' she offered. The raven seemed to be glaring at her now. 'I'm more annoyed about this than you are,' Saga told it grumpily. Bjørn huffed on her behalf. Saga sighed again. 'Which means that it was my fault that Afi and Dag were taken by the trolls?' The raven's ice-blue eyes glinted. 'What do you want from me?' Saga exploded. 'To tell you every little last detail of my life? Do you need to hear everything that I've done wrong before you let me in? Well, it was my fault that my parents died in the first place; how's that?' Saga fell into the darkest, most horrible thoughts she'd ever had and never told anyone. 'They died protecting me.'

The raven didn't move. Saga turned away, slumping in defeat as Bjørn let out a sad whimper, his dark eyes softening with worry.

Behind her came a slow creak, then a rustle of wings.

Saga turned, hardly daring to hope, but the shield doors were opening for her.

Saga gaped. 'What I said is true? It was my fault?' she whispered, horrified. Bjørn nudged her forward as Ruvsá waved, calling from the other side, so Saga pushed her terrible feelings back down and ran through with her bear.

A staircase greeted her. Its steps were hewn from ice, and it was so tall that Saga couldn't see the top of it. It disappeared into darkness. Ruvsá and Canute were waiting at the foot.

'You did it!' Ruvsá looked relieved and Saga smiled at her.

'Finally,' Canute grumbled under his breath.

Saga ignored him and looked up at the stairs. There were no railings or handles and she tried not to imagine what would happen if you slipped. Parts of it looked like a slide – impossible to walk up – but the ice had small holes and chips in it where people had climbed up with tools or weapons. On one side of the staircase was a single lantern. Its light was dying.

Saga left it there and climbed on to Bjørn's back. 'Come on.' She held out a hand to Ruvsá and pulled her up behind. 'Let's see what's inside this mountain.' She needed to find the sorcerers and get help as quickly as possible. She offered a hand to Canute, but he shook his head and pulled out a knife, carved with dragons, which he stuck into the first step and began proudly climbing up.

'Catch him if he falls,' Saga whispered to Bjørn, who slowly followed him. The staircase was no match for Bjørn's claws. With each heavy bear step, the ice groaned, but Bjørn did not slip once. It didn't take long for the lanternlight below to be gobbled up by shadows, leaving them to traverse the treacherous pass in blackness.

'We should have taken that lantern,' Ruvsá's voice echoed.

Saga winced. 'Sorry.'

'I've got it.' Ahead of them, Canute paused, wiping the sweat off his face. Holding on to his knife so that he didn't slip, he dug one of his nails into the ice and quickly inscribed a rune. White flames flared up along the step. The ice walls reflected their heatless glow, illuminating the way ahead. It was further and higher than Saga could have imagined. Behind her, Ruvsá let out a soft gasp.

'It's going all the way up inside the mountain,' Saga realized out loud. 'Are you sure you don't want to ride with us?' she asked Canute.

'And give your bear a chance to eat me? No way.' Canute sighed and began to climb again. Bjørn followed, placing his paws carefully round the flames of light.

Up and up and up.

Until Saga dared to glance over her shoulder and her vision wobbled. The staircase might have been one that clambered up to Asgard, realm of the gods, it was so long and high. She began to wonder if they would ever reach the top, if there even *was* a top or just more stairs. Yet even the longest of stories must eventually end, and so did the staircase.

CHAPTER THIRTEEN
THE GUARDIANS OF MAGIC

At the top, another door awaited them. This one was small and set deeply into the ice. Saga and Ruvsá slid off Bjørn and stood beside Canute, looking at the door. It had handles and looked like a normal door, but Saga knew that when she opened it everything would change.

'I'll probably go and sit with the warriors from my village,' Canute announced when he'd finished panting after his climb. 'They'll be expecting it, since one of us is bound to win.'

Saga barely heard him. She was too busy thinking about her afi, hoping he was all right and that the sorcerers would spring into action to save him straight away.

'What do you think it will be like?' Ruvsá asked.

This was one thing that hadn't been in her afi's stories: what the ice castle looked like. He'd told Saga it was because her mother hadn't cared about any of that; as soon as she'd seen Saga's father, he was all she had eyes for. Saga had scrunched up her face in complaint and Afi had roared with laughter. Now, Saga felt her parents' memory all around her, knowing that they had been here before. But they weren't here now; she was alone and Afi needed her. Bjørn crept closer, rubbing his big head affectionately on her as a reminder: Saga was never alone.

She opened the door.

A roar of noise spilled out of the cavernous room into which they walked. It was round with large windows cut out of the ice that peered straight down the mountain. Snow whirled in through them, piling up on the ice floor. And, now and then, a cloud wandered by – they were very, very high up. Saga's head swirled. It was curiously warm inside and sang with magic. Contestants were seated down two long tables, each one hewn from a solid block of ice. Hundreds of ice-crystal lanterns hung from the carved ice ceiling, setting everything aglow. The tables held several groups of people from all over the North, of all ages and sizes; raiders and shieldmaidens and Sámi, and some that seemed to have come from further afield, judging by the accents that mingled together like stew. A few curious glances were thrown their way, but most didn't bother looking up. Bjørn hadn't even been noticed yet.

Canute looked overwhelmed. 'We must be the last of the fifty to enter.'

'They already know we won't win,' Ruvsá murmured to Saga. 'That's why they're not worried.'

'Well, they should be,' Saga said defiantly. 'They haven't met you yet.'

Ruvsá gave her a friendly nudge. 'You mean *us*.'

'Right.' Saga's heart sank into her boots; she hadn't imagined telling the sorcerers about the troll attacks in front of so many people. Bjørn huffed, sensing Saga's distress as she looked around.

There were only a couple of other children and a handful of teenagers; most were fully fledged warriors. Saga spotted a small warband of shieldmaidens laughing and drinking from horns together, tossing their long plaited hair over their shoulders as they ignored everyone else in the hall. *They* didn't look as if they'd be scared of magic. Neither did the huddle of raiders who were telling outlandish tales of battles while devouring platters of meat. Saga dug her boots into the ice, feeling as out of place as a seal in a longhouse. She wasn't nearly as confident as she'd pretended to be to Ruvsá, and she missed her afi really badly. A man and a woman sitting alone nearby gave her an evaluating stare before their attention moved back to their meal.

Canute made a strange gulping sound. 'Do we have to go and talk to *them*?' He nodded at the centre of the hall where a violet fire floated above the ice and a raised podium held a third table. Twenty sorcerers were sitting round it, dressed in frost-blue tunics, and wearing gloves that had been scorched white with magic. Their hair was as silver as Saga's, and they'd painted themselves with runes until their skin gleamed blue. A single ice crystal dangled down over each of their foreheads, marking them as the guardians of the magic, the gatekeepers of Bifrost. A pickaxe was attached to every sorcerer's belt and if Saga squinted she could just make out the names engraved on them. Holger. Gunvald. Rollo. Vigga. Her afi had once told her about this, that the pickaxes were a symbol that, although the sorcerers stood on the highest peak of the ice cliffs to channel the magic of the Northern Lights, they also must delve deep into the caves beneath their mountain castle to chip ice crystals from the frozen stone. A reminder that their power was hard-earned and limited in supply. Saga tried not to shudder. She was a girl afraid of runes, who had walked into the beating heart of magic itself.

Steeling herself, she left Ruvsá and Canute and approached the sorcerers' table, nervously waiting until one of them noticed her. Bjørn shuffled from paw to paw, feeling her worry and frustration mounting. He stood up on his hindlegs, commanding attention. The sorcerer with the name *Holger* on his pickaxe turned to them. 'Speak.' His silver hair was cut shorter than the others and he looked more like a fisherman with his weather-worn craggy face, except for the runes inked in blue on both his cheeks.

A wave of relief swept through Saga: she was here, with the sorcerers. This marked the end of her quest. 'I came here to tell you that there have been terrible attacks across the North. Tribes of mountain trolls are raiding our villages and taking our people away,' she told him, her heart squeezing painfully at the memory of her afi, stuffed in that bone cage with the rest of the villagers.

Holger surveyed her calmly. 'Is that so?'

'Yes.' Saga drew herself taller. 'You are the guardians of magic – can you help us? My afi was taken –'

'These matters do not concern us,' Holger interrupted. 'We do not interfere in the daily business of the North. That is for your Jarls to oversee.'

Saga was aghast. 'But-but –' she stammered.

'Hurry along now.' Holger turned back to the other sorcerers.

Saga's heart fell into her boots. 'No,' she whispered. 'No! You have a duty, a-a responsibility to the North, you *must* send help!' Several of the sorcerers fell silent, watching her. Bjørn opened his mouth and roared. It shook the hall, filled with the sound of Saga's fear, her panic and awful realization that nobody was going to save her afi. Long and loud and angry and sad. Everyone fell silent.

Only the blustering wind and a distant hammering sound could be heard.

Ruvsá suddenly appeared at Saga's side. 'Come and tell me what's wrong.' She tried tugging Saga away, but Saga felt as if she'd fallen through a sheet of ice – everything was shifting around her, jagged and confusing. The sorcerers were meant to help Afi; she'd been counting on it. What could she possibly do now? She looked around in a panic. When her gaze fell on the flickering lanterns, an ice crystal embedded in the heart of each one, the seer's words rushed into Saga's head: *A hornful of ice crystals would solve your troll problem.* Of course the seer had already seen what would happen.

If the sorcerers wouldn't save her village, then that horn filled with ice crystals was the only thing powerful enough to fight all those mountain trolls.

Saga was going to have to enter the contest.

While Saga had stood there, realizing this, Bjørn was gathering a lot of attention. Saga blinked at the crashing storm of protest erupting around her. Holger stood. 'Leave the bear outside, child.'

Saga froze. She had not once considered that Bjørn would not be allowed to stay in the castle. Now that she needed to win the horn of ice crystals to save her grandfather, she couldn't leave. But neither could she send Bjørn outside this far north. He wasn't one of the white bears that stalked these islands, his fur wasn't as thick, he had never hunted nor slept outside – and she refused to choose between her grandfather and her bear.

'No,' she said.

The other sorcerers slowly turned their heads to stare at her.

'What are you doing?' Canute hissed from over by the table. 'He's a wild animal – just send him outside!'

'She can't do that. He'll freeze out there,' Ruvsá murmured under her breath.

The whole hall remained silent. Saga realized the distant hammering was probably echoing up from the ice-crystal mines, rumoured to be as deep below as the mountain peak that soared high above.

'I will do the challenges without his help and he won't hurt anyone, but we cannot be separated,' Saga added. 'He is my *fylgja*.'

Holger didn't speak for so long that Saga started to panic. She had come so far. She couldn't turn back now.

'Very well,' he said at last and sat down again. The silence shattered and Saga breathed a sigh of relief.

Ruvsá pulled Saga over to the table where Canute was sitting. Bjørn ambled along beside her, sniffing at the scents filling the air. Roasted meat and some kind of herb Saga couldn't identify. Little magical fires were dotted along the table, keeping the meat sizzling hot and cauldrons of stews and soups bubbling, but all she could think about was the contest. The terrifying, time-sucking contest in which she now must take part.

'I'm starving,' Canute moaned, grabbing a ladle and filling a bowl with stew. It steamed and scented the air with herbs and meat and earthy vegetables, and he sighed happily, oblivious to Saga's mood. As Bjørn sat at Saga's back, keeping a protective watch over her, Ruvsá piled two plates with food. She handed one to Saga. 'You'll feel better if you eat something.'

There was a variety of meat and vegetable stews that smelled so good Saga's stomach growled like a bear. There were wild mushrooms and small, sweet berries, red as jewels; huge loaves of bread, bowls of cheese and butter; platters of roasted fish and seafood; and more cakes and biscuits than Saga had seen in her life. Even as she worried about Afi and Dag and how much time the contest would take, she couldn't resist a nibble of everything while stacking a plate with roasted fish for Bjørn, who gobbled them down whole.

They feasted until another sorcerer stood.

Though their skins were different shades and there was a mixture of men, women and genderfluid people, their blue runes and silver hair marked them all as sorcerers. The one now standing was younger, his face narrow and pinched like an eagle, his eyes a sharp grey. 'My name is Rollo, and I shall be overseeing the contest,' he announced. 'You will be undertaking three challenges, each one more perilous than the last. Now that the last of our fifty have arrived –'

'How does he know that?' Canute whispered loudly to Saga. She cringed as Rollo glared in their direction before carrying on.

'The first challenge shall commence in the morning. Those that complete it will stay for the second. Those that don't will find the raven refuses to open the shield door for them.' His voice turned soft and dangerous, like a dagger wrapped in silk. 'Over the course of the contest, you shall be expected to dive into the depths of the ocean, summit the highest peaks and tread a path with death itself.'

Ruvsá nodded as if she had been expecting this. Canute tried to look equally unbothered, but his face had turned as white as the leftover fishbones.

Saga grimaced. How would she be able to do *any* of that if she couldn't use magic? But Rollo hadn't finished yet.

'Should the challenges prove too much for you, you may leave at any time, and I encourage you to do so. They are not for the faint-hearted.' He paused, surveying them all. 'Welcome to the Fifth Winter.'

CHAPTER FOURTEEN
THE FIRST CHALLENGE

When Rollo finished speaking, the biggest of the raiders let out a booming war cry and the rest of his pack joined in, banging their cups against the table. The shield-maidens laughed as the sorcerers observed silently, waiting for it to quieten down again. When the only sound was the gusting wind, he pointed towards an archway at the back of the hall.

'Choose yourself an empty room.' His grey eyes glittered. 'And choose fast or you'll be sleeping outside the mountain.'

At that, the ice benches scraped back as everyone hurried to the rooms, determined not to be tossed out into the desolate wasteland of snow and ice that awaited them on the other side of the castle doors.

Nobody was faster than Bjørn. He lolloped across the hall, with Saga, Ruvsá and Canute skidding along the ice after him. The doorway led to another dark, icy passage. 'The whole castle looks like it was carved from one giant block of ice!' Saga said as they ran ahead of the jostling crowd. Along either side of the passage were doors. Hundreds of small iron doors set into the ice. After a short run, the three children stopped at the twenty-fifth door and looked at each other.

'Did you want to –' Saga began awkwardly.

'Yes,' Ruvsá agreed, much to Saga's relief. 'Hurry inside!'

'I'm sure one of the warriors from my village will want to share with me,' Canute said quickly, as if he was afraid Saga was going to ask him to share their room as well. He vanished and Saga and Ruvsá looked at each other, their mouths twitching.

It took both Saga and Ruvsá's combined strength to shift the door open and fall inside before the crowd came racing by, searching for rooms to claim. Bjørn squeezed through just in time. Saga cast a dismayed eye over the room. 'We might as well be sleeping outside in a snowdrift,' she moaned, her teeth clattering together. 'This is an ice cave!'

It was a small pocket of a room, with low ceilings and thick walls, all made of ice. Either side of the room was an icy platform, strewn with furs for sleeping, and curling branches of ice that wrapped round each platform, tree-like. The fourth wall was carved with images of the clans of the North and the sorcerers' castle, of Bifrost, and the sorcerers overseeing all. Saga traced one of the sorcerer's flowing cloaks. 'Do the sorcerers seem strange to you?' she asked.

'In what way?' Ruvsá was examining an empty fire pit in the middle of the floor.

Saga hesitated, unsure how much to say. 'Well, my afi told me to travel to the Far North, to tell the sorcerers of the troll attack on our village, but they have refused to send any help, not even an ice crystal . . .' She shuddered, sinking deeper into her furs. 'And why is it so cold in here?'

Ruvsá hugged her arms round herself. 'C-c-c-can you cast a fire rune?' She shivered.

'Can you?' Saga bounced back.

'I'm not very good at rune magic.' Ruvsá's teeth chattered. 'I'm b-b-better at . . . other things.'

'Me too,' Saga quickly lied.

Ruvsá gave her a doubtful look as if she knew Saga was playing with the truth, but she didn't ask any more questions. A confusing mix of guilt and gratitude swirled inside Saga's head. But they were still too cold.

'You're r-r-right about the sorcerers, though,' Ruvsá added, stamping her boots up and down to warm up. 'I have a b-b-bad feeling about them. The w-w-way they looked when you asked for help –'

'Like they didn't care,' Saga said quietly, and Ruvsá nodded.

Bjørn growled a warning.

Saga lifted a finger to her lips and the two girls rushed to listen at the door. Heavy bootsteps were crunching along the ice corridor. Saga shot Ruvsá an alarmed look. When the boots hesitated outside their door, she wondered if the owner of the boots could tell that they were listening. Saga's heart clattered in her chest. Then there was a *whoomph* of light and heat, and flames suddenly shot up from the fire pit.

'A sorcerer,' Saga mouthed to Ruvsá, who nodded. The boots moved on. Saga and Ruvsá hurried to warm their hands on the bright violet fire. As if by agreement, they didn't speak about the sorcerers again, but their conversation left a bad taste in Saga's mouth.

'Why don't you trust Canute?' Ruvsá asked later when they were both nestled into their furs, watching the fire dance between their beds. It was a magical fire and though it moved like normal flames and warmed the room, it didn't melt the ice.

Saga chewed on her lip. 'How do you know that?'

Ruvsá gave a friendly laugh. 'You're not very good at hiding your feelings.'

'Well, why do you trust him?' Saga asked.

'I don't like thinking the worst of people,' Ruvsá admitted. 'It feels mean, like I'm waiting for them to make a mistake.'

'Hmm.' Saga felt a bit bad. Then Canute's smug smile and sauntering walk popped into her head and she didn't feel bad any more. He had been terrified that she'd overhear his deepest secret, he'd spent half the time acting as if he was as brave as a legendary warrior and the rest of the time he'd been afraid. And then there were all the dragons. 'He's hiding something big,' she told Ruvsá.

Ruvsá shuffled in her furs. 'I think we all are,' she whispered. 'But we all have our reasons for entering this contest and until it ends I think we should form an alliance.'

'An alliance?' Saga echoed.

Ruvsá lifted herself up on an elbow, meeting Saga's eyes across the fire. Her brown hair had fallen round her face and was gleaming in the firelight. 'You saw the way the others ignored us in the hall until they saw Bjørn. Most of them are bigger than we are, stronger than we are. What will happen when we start to win? They're not going to like that.'

Saga thought of the shieldmaidens. How fearless they'd been, laughing and throwing their braids back as if they were just feasting by the fire, not on an epic quest to win a horn of ice crystals in the coldest, most ferocious islands that existed. Then Saga thought of her own magic and how she'd never finished carving a single rune. 'I wouldn't be so sure we're going to win.'

Ruvsá slumped back. She was silent for so long that Saga wondered if she'd fallen asleep. But then – 'I have a feeling we'll do better than they think.'

Saga smiled into the dark. It was the kind of smile that curved like a dagger.

Saga didn't think she'd be able to sleep. She was far away from home, with her grandfather and best friend in danger, and now she had to win a fearsome contest against all the odds. But she'd been journeying for days to reach the sorcerers' ice castle and she was the kind of tired that burrows into your bones. She fell into a dream as deep as an ocean.

She was walking down an icy passageway, lit by green-blue lanterns. But, as she walked further into the mountain, the lanterns became further and further apart, until she was swallowed by shadows. Then, dream-Saga drew an unfamiliar rune with her finger and the green-blue light seeped out of the lanterns and gathered. It grew until it was shaped like a great bear of light. When it ran down the passageway, the ice glittered. Saga chased it. But its luminous paws were quick flashes and she couldn't run fast enough and soon darkness closed over her once more.

When she woke up, Saga was still half dreaming of bears. She and Ruvsá pulled on their boots and mittens and followed Bjørn to the great hall, hoping that the bear's twitching nose meant breakfast was being served.

It did.

Saga stopped dead in the doorway. The tables were groaning under platters of pickled herring, slices of soft cheeses and meats, loaves of freshly baked breads and steaming cauldrons of porridge. It smelled like a dream. Bjørn huffed with excitement and lolloped over.

Saga gasped and nudged Ruvsá, who was still rubbing her eyes. 'Look, fresh berries!' She pointed at the bowls of lingonberries, cloudberries and raspberries dotted over the tables. 'I haven't seen fresh fruit since autumn.' They must have been magically preserved. 'I guess there are some good things about magic after all,' she mused, nearly missing Ruvsá's eyebrows draw together.

'What do you mean –' Ruvsá began.

But Saga had spotted something else. 'No, Bjørn, that porridge is for everyone. Take your paw out of it!' She hurried over to supervise her bear as Ruvsá giggled.

Saga was eating flatbreads with honey and fruit when Canute appeared. He looked warily at Bjørn, who was gobbling down a ginormous bowl of honey-drizzled porridge, oats all over his paws and nose.

'He won't hurt you,' Saga said through a mouthful of mulched lingonberries. Canute grimaced and Saga gulped it all down. 'Sorry.'

Bjørn growled as Canute sat down. Saga gave her bear an amused glance. 'He doesn't usually dislike people this much.'

'Great,' Canute muttered, reaching for a bowl of porridge.

'Do you have any idea what the first challenge might be?' Saga asked.

At the same time, Ruvsá questioned, 'Who's sharing your room with you? Did you find your warrior friends?'

Canute paused in adding a handful of hazelnuts to his porridge.

'Answer Ruvsá's first,' Saga said, suddenly curious.

'Well –'

'There you are!' A small child popped up at the table, beaming at Canute. Canute looked as if he wished the ice would crack and swallow him whole.

Saga laughed. 'Aren't you a bit young to be a warrior?'

'I'm not a warrior – I'm Elof,' Elof said, regarding them all seriously from under his floppy brown hair. 'And I'm five and a half.'

Ruvsá handed Elof a bowl of porridge as he scrambled up to sit next to Canute. 'What are you doing entering the contest?' she asked him.

Elof gave her a wary look.

'We won't tell anyone,' Saga promised. 'Did you journey up here alone?'

Canute grumbled to himself.

'What was that?' Saga asked.

Elof giggled. 'He's just cross because my cat jumped on his face in the night.' Elof reached down into his tunic and pulled out a slightly squashed, very fluffy kitten. 'But Squirrel just likes attention. Leif didn't mind!'

'You named your kitten Squirrel?' Saga tried not to laugh. 'Wait, who's Leif?'

Canute jerked his head at the quiet couple Saga had spotted the night before. 'Him.'

'Really?' Saga peeked at them again. Leif was tall and thin and looked like a nervous mouse, and the woman was wearing her red hair in a knotted bun, braided with ribbons. 'I thought they were together.'

Canute shrugged. 'That's Unn. They're friends from the same village.'

Unn suddenly looked up. Her eyes were as green as spring, her nose as strong as a sword, and her mouth disapproving. Saga quickly turned her attention back to Elof, whose kitten had escaped his arms for the herring.

'Squirrel, no!' Elof took off after the grey ball of fluff as Bjørn emerged from his bowl of porridge, ears twitching.

'Don't even think about it,' Saga told her bear. 'We don't need any more trouble.' She turned to Ruvsá and Canute, who were discussing the first challenge.

'My brothers said we'd be hunting winged horses and wrestling captive mountain trolls,' Ruvsá said, 'but once they told me that if I collected enough feathers to make a cloak they could cast a rune to make me fly.'

'Did you?' Saga asked curiously.

Ruvsá grimaced. 'I jumped off the roof of our *lávvu* and fell straight down into a pile of snow while they nearly died laughing.'

'How many brothers do you have?' Canute asked. 'And did they all enter the contest?'

'Three,' Ruvsá said miserably. 'All older than me. Only two of them have entered and it was ten years ago. They were out by the first challenge, but, from the stories they tell, you'd think they'd won the whole thing!'

'Is that why you entered?' Saga asked. She'd never imagined having a sibling before – Dag and Bjørn had always been enough for her – but now she wondered what it might have been like.

'Yes.' Ruvsá's eyes blazed with determination. 'They all think of me as the baby of the family, someone to play tricks on or tease, to keep safe from any adventures . . . I'm going to prove that I'm just as brave as they are.'

Saga cut Ruvsá a huge chunk of cake, dripping with honey and studded with lush berries. She poured half a jug of thick cream over it. 'This will give you the energy to prove them all wrong,' she told her, catching Bjørn's paw just before it dipped into the cream. 'I'm going to take Bjørn back to our room now.'

When they'd walked back to the room, Bjørn lowered his head. Saga stroked him behind his ears. 'I know,' she told him. 'I don't like this either, but I promised the sorcerers you wouldn't help me.' Bjørn whined. 'I'll be careful.' Saga rested her forehead against his. 'And then I'll come back and we'll be together again, and maybe we can figure out what to do next. I don't know how long this contest will take, or if Afi can even wait that long, but if it's my only chance to save him then I have to do it.'

Bjørn whined again when Saga left the room, but he didn't try to follow her. She gently closed the door, leaving half of her heart behind.

When Saga re-entered the hall, Rollo was standing at the front, clasping the ice crystal on his forehead. His magic pierced the air, sharp and high-pitched, resonating through the ice and down to her bones. Saga rushed back to the table, trying not to be sick. First the sorcerers had refused to help with the trolls, and now she was plunging straight into the first challenge of the contest she'd never wanted to enter. It was shaping up to be a terrible morning and Saga wished she could close her eyes and wake up in her own bed at home.

'Are you all right?' Ruvsá whispered, and Saga nodded, shoving her fears and doubts away. Afi needed her to be strong now.

A crack shuddered through the ice. Rollo raised his arms and it splintered apart, juddering through the hall and leading to the shieldmaidens. They didn't leap out of the way as Saga thought they would but calmly pushed their bench back as a gaping hole opened up in the floor.

Several contestants exclaimed. Rollo lowered his arms with a wicked grin, as if he was enjoying himself a bit too much. 'Who would like to go first?'

'Is this the first challenge?' Saga asked in an undertone.

Ruvsá shook her head. 'Before you came in, he said that we'd have to travel to the first challenge. It's out there somewhere.' They both looked at the windows cut out of the ice and at the howling darkness beyond. Here, it wasn't like Saga's village, where even in the blackest of winters they had a few hours of gentle blue light that dappled the fjords every day. Here, every day was like the middle of the night. The purple flames of the magical fires licked higher, and Saga noticed that the windows weren't open holes after all; they were coated with a thin film of magic, like a soap bubble. It looked a little like her parents' shield, and sadness twisted Saga's stomach. It was chased with determination. She was here for a reason. If the sorcerers wouldn't help her find her afi, then Saga would have to win that horn of magic and save him herself.

'I'll go first.' Saga stood up, making Canute's mouth fall open. Rollo watched as she walked over to the hole. She peered inside, but couldn't see anything; it was a dark mouth. She hoped it wouldn't bite her. Sitting on the edge, she nodded to Ruvsá, who gave her an encouraging gesture, and then Saga let go.

CHAPTER FIFTEEN
THE WHITE-BEAR'S DEN

Fast and faster Saga slid, whizzing round twists and shooting round bends until she couldn't help laughing out loud. It was an ice flume that ran all the way down through the castle and the mountain, and it was better than sledging. Saga whooped. When the flume came to an abrupt end, she tumbled on to a pile of fluffy snow outside. She lay there for a moment, until there was a *whumpf* and another pair of boots shot out. Saga scrambled away, but she wasn't quick enough and a large fist hoisted her up by the back of her furs and sat her aside.

'Oops, nearly squashed you there,' a booming voice chortled. It was the huge raider who had led the others in the battle cry last night. He had long, braided blond hair, a nose that was bent in two places and light-blue eyes that were surprisingly friendly. His spear, shield and axe came clattering out of the ice flume behind him. 'There we go.' He picked them up, slinging his shield on to one arm and tapping it proudly. 'Never go anywhere without my sun.' His shield was wooden, reinforced with leather and painted with a cheery sun wheel. 'Name's Torben.' He clasped Saga's wrist and they shook. 'Now, who might you be?'

'I'm Saga.'

'You're a little young to be venturing so far north, Saga.' His eyes twinkled. 'I reckon you're braver than any raider I know. It's good that you are not ruled by fear like most.'

'Well . . .' Saga faltered, afraid that soon she would have to confront her fear of the runes. More and more contestants were now shooting down the ice flume and they were all grown up and confident in their magic.

Torben leaned down. 'Remember, it is not the number of raiders that seize a victory, but those who charge forward the most fiercely!' He banged his axe on his shield and strode off, joining the other raiders.

Luckily, Ruvsá and Canute appeared not long after, along with Elof, whose furs were squirming suspiciously.

Saga narrowed her eyes. 'You didn't bring your kitten with you, did you?'

'Of course not.' Elof tried to look serious, but his dark-brown eyes shimmered with mischief. A fluffy tail popped out of his collar and he pushed it back in a hurry. 'Squirrel's safe in my room,' he promised.

Ruvsá's mouth twitched as Saga struggled not to laugh.

Then Rollo shot out of the flume and landed on his feet, gracefully brushing ice from his blue robes. Without waiting to see who would follow him, he set off into the dark wilderness, away from the sorcerers' mountain. The lantern he carried flickered blue-green, like a lost wisp of the Northern Lights. Saga hurried after him, along with the rest of the contestants, who were jostling each other and making jokes, each determined to prove that they were the most fearless – apart from Leif and Unn, who kept themselves away from everyone else, conversing in whispers.

After the enchanted warmth of the ice castle, the cold was a shock. Saga's teeth chattered, she shivered and shook, and her eyelashes froze. If only Bjørn was with her, then she could nestle into his fur and bury her face in his familiar smell. He always smelled like home. But she had left him behind, so it was just Saga and the cold gnawing at her bones. Then Ruvsá skipped forward and shyly looped her arm with Saga's and some of the chill faded away.

After a long trek over the ice, Rollo stopped in what

looked like the middle of nowhere and lifted his lantern high. The contestants all craned their necks to see what this first task held for them.

'It's another hole,' Canute said.

'Like another ice flume?' Saga asked, thinking of their exit from the castle.

But Ruvsá shook her head. 'More like a white-bear den.'

Canute and Saga both stared at Ruvsá.

'Do they expect us to go down there?' Saga gasped.

'That is exactly what I expect, Saga Thorolfsdottir.' Rollo's voice slunk down Saga's spine like a shiver.

Saga frowned. 'How do you know my name?'

The lanternlight danced over Rollo's face, turning his long silver hair an eerie green. 'I have lived in this ice castle for longer than you can imagine, child. I am not merely a harvester of magic, a guardian of Bifrost – I *am* magic.' He bent closer to whisper in her ear. 'And I know all.'

Saga's heart quickened.

Rollo stepped away and raised his voice. 'As some of you have surmised, this is a bear den. There is a talisman for each of you hidden inside. You must retrieve it. Remember, the white bear of the Far North is a ferocious creature, a killer who hunts with tooth and claw, and as strong as the allfather, Odin, himself. You will enter one at a time. And you may not harm the white bear in any way.'

'Why are there not more sorcerers to bear witness to

this challenge?' Torben asked. 'How will you alone be able to tally our attempts and judge who has passed?'

Rollo's smile was ominous. Saga buried her cringe in her fluffy collar, worried for Torben.

'The other sorcerers have matters of greater importance to tend to,' Rollo said. 'They have no desire to stand outside in the cold, nor remove your bear-eaten remains. As for tallying, I can assure you I am more than up to this task, though if you continue to question me I may be inspired to . . . *forget* some of your points.'

Torben raised his shield a little at that, but said nothing. A few of the other raiders muttered something in an undertone, but none dared speak aloud. Elof's eyes had widened at the mention of *bear-eaten remains* and he was now holding on to the meowing bulge in his furs, half hiding behind Canute, while Saga was busy wondering what was so important that the sorcerers never left their ice castle, not even to watch a nearby contest taking place.

Ruvsá's arm tightened round Saga's. 'What if someone takes more than their fair share of talismans?' she asked.

'The talismans are magicked; only one will be visible to each of you.' Rollo's grey eyes gleamed under his lantern. 'We are not entirely without mercy.'

Torben stepped forward. 'Very well, then I shall go first.'

The leader of the shieldmaidens arched an eyebrow at this. 'Why should you have that honour?' She faced off against him, her armour delicately chinking together, her sword strapped to her back. What could be seen of her golden hair was braided in sophisticated patterns and her expression was fierce.

Torben stood his ground. 'I volunteered first.'

'Just because you have the loudest voice does not mean the world should bend to your will,' the shieldmaiden shot back.

Torben spluttered.

Saga glanced at Rollo to see if he would step in before someone drew their sword, but to her surprise, he looked rather entertained.

It began to snow. As the snowfall grew thicker, so did Saga's nerves. She needed to complete this task; standing out in the snow wouldn't save Afi. Before she lost her courage, she stepped forward.

'I'll go first.'

Rollo fixed his glittering stare on her. 'Are you certain you don't wish to walk away and live another day? Or will you stay to fight for the magic you need?' His smirk was knowing. It gave Saga the fire she needed to compete.

Clenching her hands inside her mittens, she ignored the murmured disappointment and scowls from the other contestants who had wanted to be first, and held her head high.

'I'm going to fight.'

CHAPTER SIXTEEN
THE FIRST TALISMAN

Saga's knees clunked together under her furs as she stumbled towards the white-bear den, losing her bravery with each step. Her breath rasped and her palms sweated in her mittens.

She was deeply afraid. Ignoring the silent crowd watching her, she climbed into the round opening.

At least nobody else could see her now.

Swivelling her head from side to side, she blew out a sigh of relief that she hadn't immediately come face to face with the white bear.

The den was empty.

But there were two more tunnels leading off from it – the space was bigger than she'd thought. A shaft of

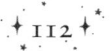

moonlight shone down into the main chamber where she stood, but the other two tunnels would be dark inside. She couldn't spot a talisman and her heart sank – she'd have to try to use magic again. Stealing over to the nearest tunnel, Saga peered inside, listening. Nothing. Holding her breath, she crawled through as fast as she could, until she felt the space open around her into another little ice chamber, where she could stand up again.

It was as dark as a moonless night.

Saga tore off one mitten with her teeth, preparing to carve a rune for light, but her hand was shaking too much, her stomach clenching. Then her eyes adjusted. There was no bear here either, though across the chamber something glimmered. Saga darted over and snatched it up, desperate to flee before the bear appeared. It was a gleaming silver coin with an engraved rune: Reið, the rune of both physical and spiritual journeys, which looked like an arrowhead with two legs, one of them kicking out as if making the first step on that journey. *The talisman.*

Magic thrummed through it, on to Saga's bare hand, and, as it did, something else flickered along her fingers: a frosted-blue shimmery light. Saga gasped, suddenly dropping the talisman. The light vanished at once.

Quickly, she pulled her mitten back on and picked the talisman up again, shoving it deep into her pocket as she turned to rush out of the den.

But the entrance was blocked by the white bear.

Saga froze. Bjørn was twice as big as she was, and she'd been expecting this bear to be the same size. It wasn't. The white bear was easily three or four times bigger than her and much wider than Bjørn too, with paws the size of Saga's head, tipped with long black claws. Saga inched backwards. Ice crunched beneath her boots.

The bear growled.

It was deep and fierce and suddenly Saga didn't know if she was more scared of the white bear or the magic she'd have to use to escape it. If she even *could* use magic; each time she'd tried, it had made her ill. She hesitated.

The bear threw back its head and roared.

Saga screamed and drew Afi's dagger.

But before she could defend herself the frosted blue light appeared again. And this time it was shimmering over all of Saga. Its magic crackled and spat, and the white bear flinched. Surveying Saga through its beady eyes, it swiped a fast paw at her. Saga leaped back too slowly to avoid its claws. She braced herself, but the claws bounced off the magic, almost like . . .

'It's the shield!' she gasped.

The white bear let out a whine that sounded too similar to Bjørn, making Saga feel guilty for the dagger she still clenched in her hand. She slid it back inside her furs, grateful that she hadn't had to hurt the bear or lose the contest before it had even properly started. The bear slunk away.

Before it clambered back into one of the tunnels, it swung its big head round, meeting Saga's eyes for one last look at the girl humming with magic. Then, it left her alone.

Saga's heart was still fluttering when the shield vanished again. Only this time, she knew her parents' last wisp of magic wasn't truly gone. It was living under her skin, ready to snap over her and protect her from any threat, just like it had done back when the trolls attacked her outside the village. Saga's throat was too thick to swallow. Though the idea of having that much magic living within her was scary, it had also felt like a hug from her parents, and that was something she had missed very much. With that thought, a bit of her fear suddenly melted away.

Aware that the bear could return any moment, Saga fled from the den.

When she reached the opening, she held the first talisman high, its rune twinkling like star glitter. Ruvsá cheered, Canute gave her a brief nod and Elof whooped.

'How . . . surprising,' Rollo said, watching Saga as she rejoined the group. 'Keep hold of that talisman, child. We shall use that to track you in future challenges. Who would like to try their luck next?' His smile revealed too many teeth. 'The bear sounds in a foul temper now.'

Elof danced from foot to foot. 'My turn next, my turn!'

'No!' Unn broke through the crowd. Her hood was pushed back, her red hair half frozen. 'This cannot be allowed – he is only a child!' She gestured at Saga, Ruvsá and Canute. 'As are those three. I am certain even the eldest boy doesn't have an arm cuff from his Jarl yet – he has not come of age. Surely there must be rules against young ones entering.'

Canute reddened. 'I *am* old enough to have an arm cuff,' he snapped.

Unn hesitated, surveying him. 'Yet you do not? There must be a reason for that.'

Saga's curiosity about Canute deepened, but she felt sorry for him. Unn was digging into his secrets in front of everybody; she would have hated that too.

Canute's voice raised in pitch. 'Nothing that concerns you! You want me to prove myself to you? Fine, watch this,' and with that Canute stomped straight into the white-bear den.

Unn gasped and clutched Leif, who drew her away. The shieldmaidens looked intrigued, and Torben and the other raiders muttered between themselves, disgruntled that they hadn't been able to go first or second to take the glory. Everyone else fell silent. And waited. Saga shuffled from foot to foot to keep warm and distract herself from Canute disappearing into that hole. Though he was annoying and she was still sure he was hiding something, she didn't want him to end up as bear dinner.

Without warning, an almighty roar shook the land. Icicles fell from the entrance of the den. The hair on the back of Saga's neck shot up.

'What was *that*?' Elof gulped, grabbing Saga's arm.

'Was that the white bear?' Saga asked Ruvsá, who looked equally alarmed.

'I'm not sure.' Ruvsá's eyebrows drew together.

With another shattering of falling icicles, Canute was suddenly rushing out of the den, his face pale but smug. He opened his mitten to reveal the second talisman.

Torben chortled. 'Looks like you underestimated these children.' He threw a pointed look at Unn, who glared at him. He then handed his spear and axe to a wolfish-looking raider with shaggy grey hair and tufted eyebrows, and leaped into the hole. His war cry echoed behind him. Nothing else was heard until he emerged from the den with dishevelled furs and another talisman.

After that, there was a steady stream of various raiders and shieldmaidens going and having a turn, cheering each other on by yelling 'Tyr!' and various battle cries, and a few contestants that seemed to be loners and had not banded together with the others. For some, like the shieldmaidens, scarcely any time had passed before they stalked back out. Others were met with the bear's wrath. Like Leif, who managed to claim his talisman but re-emerged, ashen, with three long gouges on his arm. Unn took so long Saga began to fret that Rollo would be reclaiming her body soon, but she eventually came back up with her red hair sticking out in every direction, and a talisman. A few didn't succeed and joined a growing group sitting on the snow to one side.

'When will it be my turn?' Elof demanded. 'I *have* to win the magic ice crystals!'

Saga gave him a nervous look. He was just so *small*. 'You know, that bear in there isn't like mine,' she told him as Ruvsá nodded seriously at her side. 'He's much bigger, with terribly sharp claws.'

Elof swallowed loudly. 'I'm not afraid,' he said stubbornly. 'I need the magic so I can have my own sledge pulled by a team of sled-cats. Like the goddess Freya and her chariot of cats.'

'Err . . .' Saga found herself at a loss for words.

'Cats don't really make good sled-dogs,' Ruvsá commented. 'They're not big or strong enough and they wouldn't enjoy it.'

'That's why I need the ice crystals.' Elof looked at them as if they were stupid. 'To make big magic cats.'

Canute started laughing.

'It's not funny!' Elof stamped his foot in the snow. 'Mother said I can't have more cats, but –'

'Elof.' A tall man appeared behind him. 'I thought I was having a nightmare when I saw you, but of course you're here.' He let out a long-suffering sigh.

'Hello, Filpa,' Elof said in a small voice.

Filpa was winding a strip of cloth over a badly bitten hand; he was one of the contestants who had been chased out by the bear before finding a talisman. 'I would ask how in the gods you managed to wind up in the Far North, but I have a horrible idea I already know the answer.'

'Are you from the same village?' Saga asked.

'We are.' Filpa nodded. 'This one must have sneaked on to my sledge before I left. His mother will be frantic by now.' He seized Elof's hand with his uninjured one. 'I'll be taking him home now.'

'No! What about my cats?' Elof yelled as he was pulled away. Ruvsá quickly returned Squirrel to the little boy, who clung on to his kitten as he miserably waved goodbye.

'That's a relief,' Saga said. 'Are you going to miss your warrior friend?' she teased Canute, who snorted and muttered something that sounded like '*cats*'.

'Who's next?' Rollo called out. His hawkish eyes scanned the crowd for the bear's next victim.

Ruvsá walked over. 'Me.'

She entered the den as silently as a snowflake. Saga's stomach was a thrashing sea as she disappeared into danger, but Ruvsá had barely vanished from sight when she appeared again, climbing out with a wide smile and a talisman clenched in her fist.

'How did you do that?' Saga breathed in astonishment.

Ruvsá gave her an evaluating look. 'Are we swapping secrets now, then?' she asked.

Saga clamped her mouth shut again.

When the challenge had ended, Saga looped her arm through Ruvsá's for the long trudge back to the ice castle. She couldn't wait to see Bjørn; she didn't remember the last time they'd been apart for this long and suspected that they never had been. But with the success of completing the first challenge, the warmth of walking arm in arm with Ruvsá and knowing that her parents' protective magic had never left her, Saga didn't feel alone any more.

CHAPTER SEVENTEEN
THE HOT SPRINGS

When they reached the foot of the ice flume, they were a smaller party than that with which they'd headed out. Twenty-odd contestants out of fifty had left, nursing their wounds and pride.

Rollo's ice crystal began to glow. 'One at a time, lie down at the bottom and you will be lifted back to the great hall.'

Canute cast a wary eye at the flume. 'That's a long way back up,' he said from behind Saga and Ruvsá.

'Or you may climb the ice staircase and pass the raven's test again.' Rollo shrugged. 'It is of no concern to me, though the evening meal is being served and this magic shall only last a few moments. I suggest you take advantage while you can.' And, with that, he lay at the end of the flume and promptly flew up.

There was a frantic rush.

'I don't think anyone wants to meet that raven again.' Saga pulled a face at Ruvsá, who agreed. When it was Saga's turn, she sat on the bottom of the flume and leaned back. She felt an invisible force grab her, sucking her up through the flume in reverse. With her hair on end, shooting up round the twists, she hadn't caught her breath when she popped out of the top of the flume and fell and rolled on to the ice in the great hall.

Torben came roaring after her, followed by Ruvsá.

'Odin's beard, that was a wilder ride than if I'd mounted Sleipnir!' He patted his own beard back down.

Saga laughed at the mention of the god Odin's eight-legged horse. The great hall was warm with the scent of hearty stew and she could smell bread, fresh from the fire. Pushing back her fur hood, she tried to brush the ice from her hair.

'You look like you need a dip in the hot springs,' Torben told her, 'before you turn into an icicle.'

'What hot springs?' Saga asked, Ruvsá listening at her side.

'You haven't discovered them yet?' Torben's shaggy eyebrows shot up his forehead. 'I would have thought you young ones would have explored the whole castle by now.'

'That's forbidden,' Saga said unsurely.

Torben gave her a mischievous grin. 'So don't get caught.'

Unn flew up from the ice flume at that moment, landing neatly on her feet like a cat. 'Pay no heed to Torben's teasing. The entrance to the hot springs is hidden at the back of this hall.' She pointed at a glassy wall of ice. When Saga squinted at it, she detected the outline of a door. 'Before your group arrived, the sorcerers informed us that we were most welcome to make use of it.' She glanced at Torben, her green eyes filling with concern. 'But you were right, the rest of the castle is strictly out of bounds – you mustn't go exploring or you'll be sent home and forfeit the contest. Or worse.'

Torben scratched his beard. 'I reckon you've got better ears than a cat, woman. How did you hear all that from inside the flume?'

'You happen to be extraordinarily loud, Torben,' Unn said with a roll of her eyes. 'The whales in the sea could have heard you booming away.'

'We'll only go to the hot springs,' Saga interrupted to promise, Ruvsá nodding in agreement.

'Bjørn!' Saga ran into her room, sending the door flying open and thudding into the wall as she called for her bear. Roaring his delight, he tumbled over the ice and wrapped his paws round Saga as she hugged him fiercely.

'I missed you so much,' she said into his fur. 'But look! I did it!' She pulled the talisman from her pocket, wincing a little at the gleaming rune before stuffing it back inside. After Saga had given Bjørn lots of tummy rubs, they walked into the great hall to join Ruvsá and Canute for dinner.

But as soon as Bjørn saw Canute, he sniffed uncertainly, a growl rumbling in his throat, ears tucked flat against his head.

'What's wrong?' Saga asked him in amazement. Bjørn thumped his front paws on the ice, blowing air from his nose.

'I told you he doesn't like me!' Canute yelped, hiding behind Ruvsá.

Saga frowned, wondering what had got into her bear. She waved a fish at Bjørn, distracting him from Canute, and the three children and one bear settled into their feast.

After a moose-sized bowl of stew, scooped up with rough chunks of fresh bread slathered with golden butter, and sizzling fish that had been roasted in the fire until their skins were crisp, Saga and Ruvsá made their way to the hidden door at the back of the great hall.

'I hope there won't be any sorcerers about,' Ruvsá said as Bjørn happily plodded behind them.

Saga quickly looked over her shoulder at the sorcerers' table. Rollo seemed to have more bloodlust than the most ferocious raider, and when she'd tried to tell Holger about the troll attack on her village he hadn't listened. She still hadn't forgiven them for not saving her afi and she didn't trust any of them.

'Me too,' she said darkly.

They slipped through the door unseen, following a narrow passageway that was warmer than the hall. Sconces lit their path with violet fire. As they walked deeper into the castle, melting ice from the walls and ceiling dripped down the back of Saga's neck. 'Ugh,' she shuddered, drawing her tunic closer round herself, 'I should have brought my furs for this!'

'I don't think you'll need them.' Ruvsá pointed past a nearby sconce to where the wall looked different; here it was no longer ice but rock. 'Look, this must be where the castle ends.'

'We're deep in the mountain now,' Saga agreed.

They exchanged excited looks. Not long after, they discovered low doorways cut from the rock. When they peered inside, they saw hot springs in little caves, filled with shieldmaidens and other contestants who had favoured warming up before eating. Saga and Ruvsá found an empty cave and scurried inside, Bjørn padding after them.

'Oh,' Saga said happily. 'It's hot in here.' It was probably the only place in the whole castle that wasn't made of ice.

'I'd forgotten what being this warm even felt like!' Ruvsá laughed as both girls tore off their thick overlayers and boots. 'Which hot spring do you want to try first?'

'All of them!' Saga said.

There were a variety of steaming pools of water, sunk into the rock. In a rainbow of colours, some churned like a cauldron, others were scattered with herbs and minerals, another seemed to be blowing soap bubbles by itself. One was as large as Saga and Ruvsá's room, another the size of a puddle.

Bjørn dabbed a paw in a dark-green bubbling pool.

'What do you think?' Saga asked him. Bjørn leaped into the water, sending a great wave hurtling over Saga and Ruvsá, who both squealed. Steam curled up in the air as Bjørn wallowed in the pool, making happy bear sounds.

Saga stepped in after him. Her legs sank into deliciously warm water and she walked deeper and deeper, until only her nose and eyes poked out of the steam.

Ruvsá joined her with a delighted sigh. 'So, how did you get past the white bear, then?' she asked. The ends of her long brown hair dipped into the water.

'Magic runes.' Saga shrugged, kicking out her legs and watching the water ripple as she avoided Ruvsá's eyes. 'What about you?' She glanced up curiously. 'You took almost no time at all. What happened inside that bear den?'

Ruvsá floated on her back, the bubbling water making her bob up and down. 'The bear didn't seem bothered. I just walked in and picked up the talisman.'

Saga narrowed her eyes at Ruvsá, but didn't say anything. She hadn't exactly shared her own secrets so why should Ruvsá? It felt lonely, though, and she suddenly missed Dag, who knew her as well as if she was made of ice and he could see straight through her. She hoped he was all right; she'd already been away for longer than she'd planned and she worried about what was happening to Dag and Afi with the trolls. But the seer had wanted Saga to enter the contest, so Saga had to trust that she'd made the right decision – even if winning it felt impossible.

After soaking for a while longer, the two girls and Bjørn sat on one of the large rocks around the cave, drying off on the warm stone until they could pull their overclothes and boots back on.

It wasn't until they were leaving that it happened.

Saga had cast a longing look back at the steaming pools, wondering if her parents had swum here when they'd entered the Fifth Winter, if they had been afraid too or if they were braver than her, and what secrets they'd told the raven door. She decided she liked picturing them here, hoping that some of the new memories she'd made were memories they'd had too. She'd just decided to swim in the large sky-blue pool next time, when she heard a soft song behind her, followed by a bear-like rumble. Turning round to Bjørn, she saw Ruvsá quietly sing those same notes again. And Bjørn responded.

When Ruvsá noticed Saga staring, she turned scarlet.

But Saga had already known Ruvsá's secret, hadn't she? The knowledge of it had itched at the back of her head, slowly taking root in her thoughts until just now, when everything had come together and she'd realized that she'd already known. The way Ruvsá's reindeer, Snowflake, had been so obedient. How they'd crossed a sea on whaleback, how quickly she'd completed the first challenge. Why Bjørn had instantly taken to her.

'You can speak to animals,' Saga said out loud.

CHAPTER EIGHTEEN
SECRETS AND CAKE

'Shh, not here.' Ruvsá looked around as if someone might pop up from one of the pools. 'You never know who might be listening.'

Saga nodded, questions whirling through her mind, faster than a snowstorm. She waited until Ruvsá had finished bundling up and then they walked through the rocky passageway, following it through the mountain until it turned to ice. Soon they were facing the door back to the great hall. Saga yanked it open. Cold air whistled through. It chilled Saga down to her bones. She darted into the great hall, where most of the raiders were still feasting, and then along to their room as fast as she could, Ruvsá and Bjørn racing either side of her, until she slammed the door shut behind them. It was much warmer inside, thanks to the sorcerers' magical fire. There, Saga turned to face Ruvsá. And waited.

'Yes,' Ruvsá admitted. 'I can communicate with animals. But *you're* afraid of magic.'

Saga took a step back. 'How did you know?'

'Bjørn told me,' Ruvsá simply said.

Envy bit at Saga. She had her own way of communicating with her bear, but she wished she could talk to him.

'It doesn't work how you're thinking,' Ruvsá added quickly, noticing Saga's mood change. 'We can't have a conversation together; animals don't have words like we do. It's more like feelings and sometimes images. But I noticed that whenever you were around anything magical, especially the runes, Bjørn feels nervous and concerned about you. Then I realized that I'd never seen you use magic yourself, and you avoid touching anything magical with your bare hands.' Ruvsá looked puzzled. 'But I don't understand why you'd enter this contest if you're scared of magic?'

Saga drooped. She sank down on to her bed. Bjørn let out a low whine and rested his head on Saga's lap. His familiar weight soothed her, and she stroked him behind his ears, on his favourite spot. It didn't matter if she couldn't communicate with him the way that Ruvsá could – she still knew him better than anyone. And he knew her too. Remembering this warmed her better than the hot springs.

'Because I didn't have a choice,' Saga admitted.

Ruvsá went and rummaged in her knapsack. She drew out a cloth-wrapped bundle and unfolded it to show Saga. It looked like a loaf of soft, crumbly bread, but Saga smelled apples and honey and sweet spices. Her mouth watered. Ruvsá split it into three.

'Here.' She held out one third to Saga. 'If we're going to share secrets, let's share this as well. My mother always says that difficult stories are easier to tell over cake.'

'Where did you get this?' Saga sniffed it eagerly.

Ruvsá gave her a mischievous smile. 'One secret at a time.'

Saga bit into it. It melted in her mouth and tasted of wild honey and cardamom. The apples had been magically preserved and Saga half wondered if whoever had made the cake had managed to sneak past Idun, the goddess of youth and guard of the precious golden apples that the gods ate to stay young forever. Bjørn sat up indignantly and batted a paw at Ruvsá, who laughed and offered him the biggest third. 'I haven't forgotten you – don't worry.'

Bjørn made a big happy-bear sound and his cake vanished, showering Saga with crumbs.

Saga brushed them off her tunic and took a big bite of her cake before Bjørn could gobble it down as well. 'It started when I was five.'

Saga told Ruvsá the whole story: of the first troll attack where her parents had died conjuring the magical shield that was now bonded to Saga; of the second troll attack that had been her fault, and how they'd taken her whole village away, including Dag and her afi; of the seer who had told Saga to enter the contest; and, finally, of the raven on the shield door, who'd agreed that Saga's parents had died because of her.

At that, Ruvsá shook her head hard. 'The raven didn't open the doors for you because that was true – it opened the door because *you* believed it was true, but it isn't. You can't feel guilty for your parents' choice! Look at the danger you're putting yourself into to bring your afi home – should he feel that that's his fault?'

'No –' Saga began.

'Then you shouldn't feel guilty that your parents did everything they could to protect you,' Ruvsá said firmly. 'Now I understand why you're afraid of magic –' she nodded thoughtfully – 'but I think you already know that it's your only chance to save your village, and that matters more.'

'I know.' Saga popped the last mouthful of cake into her mouth, ignoring Bjørn's sad whine at it all being gone. 'But I've been scared for so long that I don't even know where to begin! And when I *do* try, like when the trolls took Afi, it makes me sick. Sometimes I dream of runes that do strange and wonderful things, but when I wake up I don't recognize their shapes.'

Ruvsá gave Saga a curious look.

'What?' Saga licked her finger to pick up the cake crumbs. She was wondering if there'd be any leftovers in the great hall, but the sorcerers didn't seem the type to leave out snacks. Not like Afi, who never minded toasting thick slices of bread over the fire for her when she was feeling peckish.

'Come on.' Ruvsá stood and grabbed Saga's hands, pulling her up. Bjørn grumbled at his petting being disturbed, but he curled up on Saga's bed instead and started snoring. Ruvsá opened their door a crack and peered out. 'Nobody's there,' she whispered, her eyes gleaming nut-brown in the lanternlight. 'Let's go!'

CHAPTER NINETEEN
RUNEWORK

'Where are we going?' Saga whispered. In the time between their return from the hot springs and finishing sharing their stories, the hour had grown late. Though it was raven-black from when Saga opened her eyes in the morning to when she closed them at night, this darkness felt different. It was thicker and silent. No snippets of conversation nor barks of laughter echoed from other doors, no scents of roasted meat with herbs and spices trailed from the great hall. It was the kind of night through which not even the gods could have seen.

'To practise your magic,' came Ruvsá's reply as they passed a glowing lantern.

Saga halted.

But Ruvsá wove her arm though Saga's and tugged her further down the icy warren. 'If you want to win the contest, you must.'

'Why are you helping me? Don't you want to win as well? And why can't we practise in our room? If we get caught . . .' Saga trailed off.

'Some things are more important than winning.' Ruvsá's eyes twinkled. 'Besides, who says I'm going to let you win? Though it would be a lot lonelier in this castle if you can't even make it past the second challenge.'

Saga laughed.

'So I'm going to help you practise. Away from our room, somewhere that the other contestants won't overhear us. I will guard your secret as safely as treasure,' Ruvsá told her, squeezing her arm.

'Thank you.' Saga felt as if she had a clump of porridge in her throat. She cleared it quietly.

Ruvsá led her down to a level beneath the great hall, past a cavernous cooking space that housed several large hearths and salted fish drying, and into a small ice cave burrowed behind it. It was cooler in here, lit by a single lantern hanging from the low ceiling, the floor piled with a soft layer of snow. Pots of all kinds of food were stacked high and Ruvsá grinned, opening one to show Saga a stash of oat biscuits. 'This is where you got the cake from?' Saga guessed, popping a couple of biscuits into her pockets. They'd make a nice treat for Bjørn when he finished napping. A third biscuit went into her mouth.

'Whatever you think about sorcerers, they put on a good feast,' Ruvsá said, helping herself to the biscuits. 'But they don't seem to understand snacking.'

Saga nodded emphatically. 'I had the same thought!'

They giggled together. Then Ruvsá looked at Saga expectantly.

Saga looked back at her. 'What?' She swallowed her mouthful of biscuit.

'Well?' Ruvsá gestured.

Saga pushed up her sleeve. As she reached down to draw a rune into the snow, her hand trembled. Nerves thrashed in the pit of her stomach as if she was caught in a storm at sea and she felt sick and dizzy. She dragged in a ragged breath – and heard the unmistakable sound of a boot scuffing the ice outside. Saga grabbed Ruvsá and pulled her behind a barrel of mead. They stood almost nose to nose as Saga tried not to breathe, listening as hard as she could. Saga saw for the first time that Ruvsá looked scared, and Saga bit her lip, worried that they'd trodden a dangerous path, that this would mean the end of the contest for them both, leaving no way for Saga to rescue her afi.

Footsteps crunched into the snow. The person was entering the storage cave.

Ruvsá's eyes widened and, this close, Saga could make out tiny flecks of green and gold that shimmered like tiny jewels in her eyes. She could also see her own face reflected. Saga's silver hair was gleaming under the lanternlight shining down from above. She tugged up the hood of her tunic, trying to hide it, but the person in the room stopped.

It was so quiet she could hear them breathing.

Saga closed her eyes, pleading with the gods not to let it be Rollo. Maybe another sorcerer wouldn't be as strict or would let them go with a warning, but Rollo was much too mean to do that.

And then the person spoke. 'Saga? Ruvsá? I know you're in here.'

Ruvsá slumped in relief. All the breath came rushing out of Saga's lungs. She whirled out from behind the barrel and glared at Canute, standing in the middle of the cave.

'Why were you following us?' she demanded.

Ruvsá popped out too, giving Canute an admonishing look. 'You scared us!'

'Sorry.' Canute dug the toe of his boot into the snow. 'I was just wondering where you were going. You know we're not allowed to go off on our own in the ice castle –'

'So then why did you follow us?' Saga repeated, still annoyed.

Canute shuffled from foot to foot. 'Er –'

Ruvsá and Saga stared at him.

'I was bored!' He blushed, looking at his feet. 'Now that Elof's gone, I'm left alone sharing a room with Leif, who's never there unless he's asleep and then he snores louder than a moose.' He shrugged. 'I thought it would be more interesting to see what you two were doing so I went to knock on your door and that's when I saw you sneak out ... What are you doing?' He glanced up, curious.

'Nothing,' Saga said.

'Helping Saga practise her magic,' Ruvsá said at the same time.

'Ruvsá!' Saga exclaimed. 'That was a secret!'

'No, the other stuff is a secret that I would never tell,' Ruvsá promised, 'but he doesn't need to know that part. Besides, I'm not very good with runes – maybe he can help.'

Saga scoffed. 'He won't want to help.'

'I can help,' Canute said eagerly. 'Let's start with the basics.' He kneeled on the snow and drew a rune that looked like a lightning bolt. 'Sól,' he said as it beamed with light.

'I already know the basics,' Saga said a little grumpily. She didn't add that she'd never practised those basics herself before. Or that seeing that glimmer of magic turned her cold.

Canute rubbed the rune out with his boot, extinguishing the light. 'Then it's your turn.' He looked happier than Saga had ever seen him. And much less annoying. He was even ignoring her grumpiness. She eyed him, unsure why he was acting differently but then he gave her a wary smile and she gave in and kneeled beside him.

Her heart beating harder and harder, Saga began drawing her first rune: Sól, the little lightning bolt that she'd seen beam with the power of a summer sun when her mother drew it. One line, then another. Her breath rushed out in cold wisps as she bit her tongue, trying to ignore her stomach rolling, the cave tilting around her as she saw stars. Then she felt a hand on her shoulder: Ruvsá.

'Keep going – you're nearly there,' she told Saga, who swallowed her fear and kept drawing, knowing that the only way she could save her afi was by embracing the magic from which she'd fled her whole life.

'So close now,' Canute added as Ruvsá squeezed Saga's shoulder, the pair of them encouraging her as she finally finished her very first rune.

It hummed to life as Saga slumped down, exhausted from battling her fear. But it wasn't the bright hum of the sorcerers' runes around the ice castle, nor the quiet fierce hum of her afi's runes that had marked their longhouse. No, this was a tiny, weak hum that she had to strain to hear. Saga, Ruvsá and Canute all looked at the dim flicker of her light.

Saga's emotions were warring. 'That's it?' She was torn between astonishment that this was all she'd managed to produce after her fear about wielding magic that was as raw and powerful as her mother's, and a secret disappointment that maybe she wasn't worthy of having a magical destiny after all. Maybe the seer had got the wrong person or accidentally knocked on the wrong door all those years ago?

'You just need more practice,' Ruvsá said gently. 'It was your first time carving a rune and your hand was shaking badly.' She looked at the wobbly edges of the rune.

But Saga wasn't listening. 'How am I going to do the next challenge now?' she wailed. 'My parents' shield is defending me, but it's not going to help me with anything else.'

'That was the first rune you've ever used?' Canute frowned, his forehead wrinkled with confusion. 'And what shield?'

Saga narrowed her eyes at him.

'You don't have to tell me,' he said quickly, 'but I'm sorry if I wasn't that friendly before. I was just nervous about the contest and I wasn't sure who I could trust. My parents told me never to trust anyone,' he added, 'so I'm not used to . . .'

'Not used to what?' Ruvsá asked.

'Having friends,' Canute said in a small voice.

'We're not your friends,' Saga said, and he flinched. She closed her eyes, her stomach swimming in guilt. 'But maybe we could be,' she told him. 'Do you promise not to tell a single soul if I tell you something?' He nodded fiercely. 'Not one other person,' she repeated, 'or I'll let Bjørn eat you for dinner.'

'You have my oath,' Canute said. They grasped each other's forearms and shook on it before Saga told him a briefer version of the story she had already shared with Ruvsá earlier that night.

'Hmm,' Canute said after she'd finished. 'Maybe your parents' shield is blocking your own magic? But I wouldn't know how you'd get rid of it . . . and it did stop that white bear from eating you so it could be useful with whatever we're facing next.'

'I don't think it's blocking her magic,' Ruvsá said. 'She could walk through it when it was on the mountaintop, so it wasn't blocking her then. Try another rune.'

Now that she was distracted, Saga carved a second rune without feeling sick or dizzy.

It produced the same weak effect as before: a flicker of dull light.

Ruvsá beamed at her.

'What?' Saga looked at the rune to see what she was missing. 'It isn't any better than the first one.'

'You're so distracted by your runework that you've forgotten to be scared of them.' Ruvsá pointed at the rune. 'Your hand barely shook when you carved that one into the snow. Look how much smoother it is.'

She was right. Though that didn't solve Saga's problem – she'd assumed all along that her fear was stopping her from drawing runes, but now it looked as if she'd never had the kind of power that she'd need to even compete in the Fifth Winter, let alone win the whole thing. She'd secretly hoped that she'd turn out to be powerful enough to be able to leave the sorcerers' ice castle and go and rescue her afi and Dag all by herself, but now she definitely needed to stay in the contest. She dragged her feet on the way back to their rooms, wallowing in despair until she felt as if she was drowning.

CHAPTER TWENTY
THE NORTHERN LIGHTS

Saga didn't feel much better the following day at breakfast. Even Bjørn sticking his nose and paws in a pot of honey didn't make her smile.

'You did the first task – you can do this one,' Ruvsá told her, decorating a bowl of porridge with berries and hazelnuts and thick cream for Saga, and urging her to eat.

Saga groaned and rested her head on the table.

'Good morning,' Canute said brightly when he came and sat with them, reaching for some toasted rye bread and spreading it thickly with butter.

'Is it?' Saga moaned.

Canute waved his toast. 'Any day that starts with a feast is a good day.' He piled his plate high with cake and berries. 'This is like Jul every day!' He popped off the bench to go and fetch a glass of warm milk.

Saga's heart twinged. She'd forgotten that Jul was creeping closer. In the middle of every winter, when the darkest, shortest day came to pass, they celebrated Jul. Saga and her afi would decorate their longhouse with boughs of evergreen trees, holly and mistletoe, and there would be bonfires and feasting in the village, where they would all sing and play games. At the end, they'd set a giant wreath on fire and throw it down a mountain, to wish for the sun to return. It was Saga's favourite day of the year and usually she'd already be looking forward to it with Dag, but this year her village was empty and she was far from home.

'Hey!' Canute suddenly exclaimed, returning to discover Bjørn sitting in his place in front of a now empty plate, with crumbs all over his nose.

Saga stifled a giggle. 'That wasn't very nice, Bjørn,' she told her bear, who huffed out what sounded like a laugh and lunged for Canute. Canute squealed and dropped his milk, which Bjørn lapped up eagerly.

'It's because he knows you're scared of him,' Saga told Canute, who was scowling at Bjørn. 'You really need to learn how to hold on to your food better.' Although she suddenly remembered that after the first challenge, Bjørn had been scared of *Canute*, and she puzzled over that again.

Ruvsá nudged Saga, nodding at Rollo, who had started speaking.

'The second challenge won't take place until tonight,' Rollo announced. 'You may spend the day here, in your rooms or in the hot springs. I ought not need to remind you that any other location in the ice castle is strictly prohibited. Though I suggest you spend your day wisely –' his hawkish gaze flitted over them all – 'as the challenge that awaits you is perilous and who knows who shall walk away from it unscathed.' This time, when he sat down, the great hall did not break back into their discussions and laughter. This time, it remained silent.

'Is it just me or are the sorcerers a bit . . .' Saga hesitated.

'Creepy?' Canute offered.

'Strange,' Saga finished.

The three children and Bjørn were sitting together down in the hot springs, eating their way through a pile of biscuits Ruvsá had pinched from the storage cave, and dangling their feet in a bright berry-pink pool.

'Rollo really seems to like the idea of us failing –' Ruvsá began.

'Or being horribly killed or torn to pieces by one of his tasks,' Saga interrupted, making Canute snort into his biscuit.

'But he's the only one who's really spoken to us so far,' Ruvsá carried on. 'The others are just –'

'Creepy,' Canute interrupted.

'Silent,' Ruvsá said, throwing a biscuit at him.

'It just seems odd to me that though the sorcerers are the guardians of Bifrost and harvesters of magic, they never do anything to help anyone,' Saga thought out loud. 'They have the power to stop the troll raids or send aid when villages have been flooded or had a fire or their crops failed, but they don't. They don't even know what our lives are like!' Saga began to get heated. 'They just live up here in their ice castle, playing with magic and never bothering to use any of that magic to make our lives better. So why should they be the ones who get to make all the rules over what we can and can't do?'

Canute shrugged. 'What can we do? That's just the way it is.'

'The Sámi have known this for a long time,' Ruvsá pointed out. 'Most of us do not accept the sorcerers' laws but follow our own leaders instead.' She grinned. 'I am only here to take some of their magic from them.'

Bjørn chose that moment to amble over and steal Canute's biscuit from his hand. Canute yelped, jumping so hard that he slipped and fell into the berry-pink pool with all his clothes on.

'I told you you needed to hold on to your food better!' Saga giggled. Canute looked outraged. His hair and his nose were dripping water, and his clothes were so wet and heavy that it took him three tries to pull himself out of the pool. Bjørn huffed in delight at the biscuits Canute had suddenly abandoned, chomping them up one by one, while Saga and Ruvsá laughed until their sides hurt.

Saga dragged a finger through the snow, confidently drawing the twists and turns of a complicated rune. It looked like a bear with lightning-bolt fur. A bear touched by Baldr, god of light. No sooner had she finished than from the snow rose a luminous bear. Brighter than starlight, it ran over the snow, lighting Saga's path ahead as, far in the distance, someone called her name.

'Saga? Saga!'

'Follow the bear,' she mumbled.

'Saga, you're dreaming!' Canute shouted, and Saga woke up from her nap with a start.

'It's time for the second challenge – we need to hurry,' Ruvsá called over her shoulder as she grabbed her hood and bundled herself in extra furs.

'What were you dreaming about?' Canute asked curiously.

But Saga shook her head and turned to Bjørn instead. Leaving him again wasn't any easier the second time, and she was almost grateful that they had to rush out of the room, slipping down the ice corridor as they ran to the great hall.

But it was already empty.

There was not a whisper nor sign of the ice flume vanishing from sight like it had after the last time they'd used it.

'Did we miss it?' Saga exchanged horrified looks with Ruvsá and Canute. There were around twenty contestants left after the first task and not one of them was anywhere to be seen.

An old sorcerer shuffled into view. Her shoulders were hunched, her blue robes puddling at her feet, her silver hair as sparse on her head as snow on the mountaintops come summer. Her pickaxe bore her name in gold: Vigga. When she noticed the three children standing alone in the hall, Saga braced herself. Vigga's was the only pickaxe she'd seen with gold on it – she must be one of the elders of the sorcerers, someone very important.

Her face cracked like a nut as she smiled at them. 'Do not fear, young ones. You are not too late. The sledge is awaiting you outside.' She pointed a twisted finger at the windows. 'Run along now.'

Saga wasn't sure if she was serious – surely she didn't mean for them to jump out of the window? – but Saga dashed over to where the sorcerer was pointing anyway.

The faint purple film that usually covered the windows was missing. Saga stuck her head outside to get a better look. A fierce wind howled at her and she burrowed deeper into her furs, her eyes watering. 'There's a ledge!' she told Ruvsá and Canute, who were right behind her.

Hesitantly, she stepped out of the window and on to the narrow ledge. It was coated with thick ice and she wished she had claws with which to cling on as she carefully looked for what Vigga might have been talking about.

'There's nothing here –' She stopped, noticing something hanging from the ledge. It was a rope ladder, matted with snow, and twisting in the wind. When Saga looked down, the wind whipped more snow into her eyes and she couldn't see where it led. She glanced back at the great hall.

'Go on,' said Vigga, gesturing.

Saga stepped on to the ladder. It shuddered under her boots, threatening to fly away in the wind. When she'd descended a few shaky steps, Canute started climbing down, followed by Ruvsá, and their combined weight helped hold it steady.

As Saga descended, the glow of the castle suddenly vanished and freezing mist rushed past her face: she was inside a cloud. It tasted like snow and smelled like the sea, and she imagined it wandering in from the coast, heavy and salty. The next time Saga looked down, she almost fell off the rope ladder. A huge sledge had suddenly become visible.

Carved from what looked like the wood of fifty ancient trees, it had iron runners for cutting through the ice, a wooden roof gleaming with blue runes, and large lanterns hanging down to light its way. It hovered in the air.

One by one, Saga, Canute and Ruvsá jumped down on to its deck.

'There you are!' Torben exclaimed in his booming voice, his blue eyes shining from deep within his fur hood. 'Fenrir here was beginning to think you'd scurried off home, but I told him those young ones are braver than Tyr on a battlefield!' He clapped Fenrir hard on the back, beaming at the children. Fenrir was the wolfish raider Saga had noticed a few days ago, always slinking along at Torben's side, with lots of shaggy grey hair all over his head and face. 'Come to the fire,' Torben continued, waving his shield around to clear some room. It bumped into the leader of the shieldmaidens' leg, and she scowled at him. 'Whoops, sorry about that, Solveig,' he said. She prowled off, flipping her long, blonde braids over her shoulder, and Torben grinned. 'As you can see, she's taken to me like an eagle to herring.' Fenrir huffed a laugh and Canute snorted.

The sledge suddenly jolted. Saga and Ruvsá held on to the posts supporting the wooden roof above them.

'What was that?' Canute asked, wide-eyed.

'We're on our way now,' Fenrir said ominously, the firelight tossing shadows over his hairy face.

Purple, smokeless flames rippled down the centre of the sledge, but Saga stood near the back with Ruvsá, watching their flight away from the mountain. They flew over the snow like a great seabird, leaving silvery tracks behind in the air. Lanterns dangled from the tips of the curved runners, illuminating their path. Not long after they'd left, a brutal gust of wind came howling over the snowy plains and chased all the clouds away. As the last wisps of cloud fled, Saga gasped at the sight above: the black sky was swollen with stars. All the stories her afi had told her came rushing back and she suddenly heard his voice as if he was standing next to her, telling tales of the sun on her sky-path, of the ship-palace of Njord, god of the sea, of the frost giants who lived high in the mountains, safely tucked away in their own realm of ice, Jötunheimr, awaiting their next battle with the gods who lived in their home of Asgard. Saga wished her afi was here now. He was brave and wise, and he always knew the right thing to do. He'd told her to journey to the Far North, but he'd believed that the sorcerers would be able to help and now Saga knew that they never would. She glared in their direction. Rollo and Holger stood at the front of the sledge, guiding their passage, their ice crystals glowing brightly on their foreheads.

Saga was tempted to march over and demand they did something about the troll attacks again when the sky filled with colour. The Northern Lights were dancing.

'Look!' Ruvsá pointed back at the ice castle. Saga squinted, just making out a thin line of blue robes: sorcerers on the very tip of the mountain, high above the ice castle. Now and then the Lights pulsed brighter, surging in moss-green and sunrise-pink, before dimming. It reminded Saga of huge whales that burst out of the fjords, sending water scattering like jewels, before slowly sinking out of sight.

'It's the sorcerers,' Torben told her, looking up with Saga and Ruvsá, 'sucking the magic from the Lights to fill their ice crystals with magic.'

Saga frowned. She hadn't imagined it to be like this, as if the sorcerers were greedily feeding on the Lights, stealing the magic. 'Will the Lights ever run out?' she asked him.

Torben shrugged. 'That is a question for the gods and seers.'

Saga watched the Lights shimmer. And, beyond that, a secret glimpse of something burning bright and colourful: Bifrost, the bridge to Asgard, the world of the gods. Saga had never seen it before. She sucked in a breath, overwhelmed with wonder. And not a little curiosity.

'Do you think the sorcerers ever try to cross it?' she whispered. It was said that no mortal could set foot on it, but the sorcerers didn't act like normal people and nobody knew how powerful they really were.

'They'd be fools if they did,' Unn replied, startling Saga, who hadn't realized she'd joined them to watch. She gave Saga a funny kind of smile. 'Then again, show me a man who has never acted like a fool.'

Not sure what to say, Saga glanced back, but the bridge and ice castle were too distant to see now. She wondered how exactly the sorcerers stole the magic from the Northern Lights to fill their crystals, and why it was so important to them. The sledge hurtled onwards, the Lights rippling in pale greens and pinks, filling the sky and reflecting on the frozen wilderness. Other contestants began to grow tired of standing and sat around the fire, passing the time with tales of wars and gods, but Saga stayed at the back of the sledge, watching the rugged landscape soar by beneath, passing herds of wild reindeer, and the odd lone white bear, nearly invisible in the snow until it raised its head, black eyes glinting with reflections from the sledge's lanterns.

After a time, they reached the end of the island.

'We have arrived.' Rollo stopped the sledge. When Saga jumped down, deep snow swallowed her up to her knees. Ruvsá and Canute landed beside her, also eyeing the water that thrashed the shore, wild and inhospitable. Patches of frozen sea ice rocked on the surface. Saga really, *really* hoped their task wouldn't have anything to do with the sea.

Canute made a strange gulping sound and Saga suddenly remembered his fear of water, but her mouth was too dry to speak.

'These waters are home to giant horned whales,' Rollo began when everyone had clustered together on the shore. Saga's worry churned into dread as the sea roiled and spat at them, like a cornered beast. 'You shall be mastering your command of magic to hunt for a lost whale tusk beneath the waves. Yet take heed you do not enter these waters lightly, for they are treacherous, and many a brave contestant has frozen in their depths. Now do ensure you have tightly fastened your talisman to yourself –'

'So that you may retrieve the bodies of those that do not survive?' Unn interrupted with a roll of her eyes, making Saga gape at her. Who was this woman who was courageous enough to show such disrespect to the sorcerers?

Rollo's mouth tightened until it nearly disappeared. 'So that we may track your attempt at completing the task. If you do not feel sufficiently prepared to battle the water, then I suggest you do not enter it.'

'I believe I'm sufficiently prepared for whatever surprises you may have in store for us, across the islands *or* lurking in the halls and passageways of your castle,' Unn bit back.

'I like her,' Ruvsá whispered to Saga, who nodded fiercely. Maybe Unn wasn't so bad, after all. But Rollo did not look amused. An unreadable emotion flickered across his face as he stared back at Unn. Leif took advantage of Rollo's loss for words and seized Unn's arm, ushering her away from the sorcerer she'd deliberately provoked.

'What was that about?' Saga wondered out loud.

CHAPTER TWENTY-ONE
CANUTE'S SECRET

Saga stared at the sea, her heart thudding. Her tiny flares of magic were no match for these crashing waves and freezing depths. Even if her parents' shield could save her, it wouldn't save Afi from the trolls. The first challenge had taken out more than half the contestants and this one was bound to be harder.

'You can do this,' Ruvsá murmured at her side. But when Saga turned to reply she realized that Ruvsá was talking to Canute. Canute, who looked as if he might snap in half like an icicle, frost-white with fear and shivering as he stared at the slippery darkness. And though she was scared too, Saga reached out and held Canute's hand. She didn't think he would hold it back, but he gripped it tightly and whispered, 'I can't do this.'

'Scared, are we?' Rollo's grey gaze fixed on their hands. 'Perhaps you children ought to turn back now before you come to any real harm.' His smile was thin.

Torben snorted. 'I think they've more than proven their mettle,' he declared, gesturing at Canute as he added, 'Why don't you go first and show the good sorcerer what you're made of?'

Rollo looked sceptical.

Canute looked as if he was going to faint.

Rollo signalled to Holger, who removed an ice crystal from his pocket and drew on its magic to conjure two curving lines of purple flames that rushed around the shoreline, meeting in the middle with a crackle of magic. 'So that we may all watch your endeavours,' Rollo said. The ice crystal turned dull once drained of magic, like an ordinary pebble, and Holger tossed it away.

Saga frowned. 'Don't the sorcerers work hard to dig those out of the mines?' she whispered to Ruvsá, who nodded, a flash of wariness passing over her face. Saga felt as hot as the purple flames dancing nearby; she couldn't believe that not only had the sorcerers refused to help with the troll attacks, they were also wasting powerful magic on silly things. The sorcerers claimed that they were too busy working hard in the ice-crystal mines beneath their castle to bother with troll attacks or overseeing the Fifth Winter contest, but it didn't seem like they were *that* busy. And they must have more than enough ice crystals if they were throwing away empty ones like Holger just had!

Then Canute moaned with fright and Saga turned her focus to him. 'You faced the white bear and got the talisman,' she reminded him in an undertone. 'You still haven't told us how, but I'm guessing that your huge secret has something to do with it,' she teased. She was surprised that his secret had stopped bothering her as much as it had when they'd first met, but she supposed that becoming friends with somebody meant that you accepted them for who they are, and you didn't ask questions about things they weren't ready to share yet. Saga knew herself how difficult questions could feel like all the air had been sucked out of your lungs. She'd spent years dancing away from questions about her parents, about why she never carved runes . . .

A tiny smile flickered on Canute's face. 'But we're not in an ice den here. If I reveal my secret –' he gulped – 'everyone will see.'

'If you don't, you might drown,' Ruvsá said helpfully.

'Ruvsá!' Saga exclaimed as Canute made another strange moaning sound.

'Fine, fine! I'll go first, get it over with.' Canute was sweating now, his eyes wild moons. 'But you both still have to be friends with me after, OK?'

'We will be,' Saga and Ruvsá both promised. It was the first time Canute had properly called them his friends. They only had each other on this vast, desolate island, far from home, and if it hadn't been for Ruvsá and Canute, Saga would have spent a lot more time worrying about Afi and trolls and runes, and a lot less time eating cake and hopping into bespelled hot springs. If it hadn't been for them, she still might not have drawn her first rune.

'Good.' Canute took several deep breaths and stepped up to the edge of the water.

Torben nodded enthusiastically. 'Tyr!' he roared out, slamming his axe against his shield. Fenrir took up the rhythm, thudding his spear into a rock beneath the snow, then the rest of the raiders joined in, their drumming reminding Saga that this was a battle and soon it would be her turn to fight.

Canute looked at the water. Then he began to peel his outer layers off. As Saga peeped between her fingers, she saw his back begin to *change*. Glistening red patches emerged. 'Is he growing *scales*?' she asked Ruvsá.

Before the girls could figure out what that meant, Canute jumped over the ice. Saga sucked in a breath and Ruvsá yelped and grabbed her arm as Canute arrowed straight down and vanished in the black water.

There was a long silence. Nobody spoke and they couldn't see or hear anything in the water, even though the shallows were clear and illuminated with the sorcerers' magical fire. Not even a bubble. Then the surface of the deeper water shattered like glass.

A dragon burst up through it.

It was slender and twisting, with crimson scales that glowed like embers, a pair of membranous wings, two horns that perched atop its long, narrow head, and claws fiercer than Saga had ever seen.

She stumbled back with shock, nearly falling in the snow.

The raiders and shieldmaidens took up defensive stances at once, shields raised, spears and swords pointed up at the huge beast that had flown out of the water. Its scales matched the pattern that had spread over Canute's back. Unn's, Leif's and a few of the stragglers' mouths had fallen open, but the sorcerers seemed unsurprised. As did Ruvsá. 'This explains that roar I couldn't understand when he went inside the bear den,' she explained to Saga.

'What do you mean this explains it? This explains nothing!' Saga gaped at the dragon. 'How in the nine realms did Canute turn into *that*?'

A whale tusk was clamped between its jaws. With a shimmer and a twinkle of magic, the dragon melted away until it was just Canute standing there. He picked up the whale tusk that had fallen from his dragon mouth and handed it to Rollo, who calmly instructed him to wait on the sledge with Holger. Everyone silently watched as he walked over to Saga and Ruvsá, pulling on his outer layers as the last glowing red scales seeped back into his skin. Distrustful mutters and strange looks were shot at him like arrows, and Canute hunched over more and more, as if he could disappear.

Saga's head was spinning.

'Your turn.' Canute gave her a small smile.

'I know I can't do *that*,' Saga pointed out.

But Canute shook his head. 'Your turn to face your fears,' he told her. 'A little magic is better than no magic.' He shivered then, his clothes still wet. 'I'll be watching from the sledge.'

Before she could talk herself out of it, Saga shrugged off her furs, held her breath and jumped in.

The water was so cold it felt like broken glass. Sharp and painful. She guessed she was supposed to use a warming rune to keep it from turning her flesh stiff and lifeless; it was already difficult to breathe from the shock, but before she could attempt anything, her skin glowed a faint blue as her shield shimmered to life. It protected her from the worst of the cold, and she warmed at once. Enough to start looking around. A lost whale tusk. There were twenty-three contestants left now, including her, and only Canute had taken a turn. That meant there were twenty-two tusks scattered around the bottom of the seabed, and she only needed one. But the water was black. Remembering how Canute had burst out of the water in his dragon form, baring his secret to everyone, Saga forced herself to be brave. She'd carved her first runes now without them making her ill – she could do it again.

Steeling herself, she made the shape of the little lightning bolt, Sól, in the water. The rune for light. A tiny glow flickered in front of her, but, once more, it vanished as quickly as it had appeared. Saga grunted with frustration. She surfaced to refill her lungs with cold, pure air. Then she ducked back down and shaped the rune again.

Like last time with Ruvsá and Canute, the second attempt was easier. But the magic was as tiny as the first flash of light had been and she was immediately plunged back into the darkness with only the shimmer of her shield to see by. Sadly, it wasn't enough light to hunt for a whale tusk with. Saga's fear began to shapeshift like Canute had. Only, instead of turning into a dragon, her fear turned into frustration that her magic was so small it could never make a print on the world. Did that mean that she could never make a difference? Never save her afi?

Her chest tightening, Saga was forced back to the surface for more air. When she plunged underwater again, she tried a different rune. One that she didn't have a name for because she'd only seen it in her dreams. One that looked like the body of a bear, with four lines for legs, and jagged lightning for fur.

Light soared from her rune.

Just as in her dream, it formed a bear made out of dazzling light that glittered like snow. Saga almost sucked in a mouthful of water in her surprise and delight. The bear turned and ran through the water. Saga swam after it. Deeper and deeper it danced, now and then stopping to wait for Saga to catch up, until they had reached the seabed, where the light-bear rested a luminous paw on a long, thin spiral. A whale tusk. It was twice as long as Afi's sword. When Saga picked it up, struggling to swim back with it, the light-bear began to dim. She kicked harder, her chest squeezing painfully, her head pounding, as the light-bear faded away. When she broke the surface and gulped in big greedy lungfuls of air, it had vanished.

But everyone was staring at her.

CHAPTER TWENTY-TWO
THE LIGHT-BEAR

Saga dug her fingers into the ice and dragged herself out of the water. She was met by silence.

'Interesting.' Torben frowned to himself as Saga dropped her whale tusk alongside Canute's. The shield-maidens tracked Saga's path back to Ruvsá like a hunting eagle. She felt horribly self-conscious as she showed another of her secrets; her shield was still humming around her, preventing her wet clothes from freezing solid.

Rollo did not react. 'Next contestant,' he snapped.

'Go and warm yourself by the fire. Keep Canute company.' Ruvsá pressed Saga's hands in hers. 'I'll go next and then we can talk all together.' She paused to smile, a big smile that lit up her face from within. 'You did it, Saga!' She squeezed Saga's hands one last time and stepped forward to volunteer.

Rollo sneered at that. 'Another child? It seems that the burly raider was right: the children here do possess more courage than the warriors.'

The waves closed over Ruvsá's head and Saga was overcome by an unsettling sense of dread. But Canute was gesturing at her from the sledge and she tore herself away to join him, shrinking under the whispers and glances targeting them both, particularly him. The boy who had slipped into a dragon skin.

On the sledge, Holger was heating a cauldron of soup over the fire. If it wasn't for the runes on his cheeks and his sorcerer's robes, he would have looked quite at home with the fisherfolk in Saga's village. Saga took a bowl and joined Canute, who was huddled in a corner.

'I'm not sure it's safe here,' he whispered to her. 'The way they all looked at me afterwards . . . and now you too.'

Saga was tired after that magic had flooded out of her. Canute noticed and passed her a chunk of bread to scoop up her soup. As if by silent agreement, they didn't speak until Ruvsá joined them shortly after. She took a bowl of soup and the three of them warmed their mittens on their bowls, hot steam clouding up and tickling Saga's nose. Her shield had retreated now, sensing it was no longer needed. The magical fire was filling the sledge with smokeless heat that was quickly drying their hair and clothes.

'What was that?' Ruvsá sounded impressed. Despite a little shudder at the force of the magic that had exploded out of her, Saga couldn't help grinning. That magic had saved her, had proved to all those raiders and warriors that she was more powerful than any of them. Best of all, it had shown Saga herself that she actually stood a chance of winning this contest and saving her afi. Her grin faltered. If she did win, it meant that Ruvsá and Canute couldn't win.

But . . . Canute could turn into a *dragon*.

'I don't know,' Saga said honestly. She turned to Canute. 'Why didn't you tell us that you could turn into a dragon?' She suddenly realized that Bjørn had sensed there was something more to Canute. Her bear must have smelled the dragon on Canute after the first challenge.

'It was amazing!' Ruvsá added.

Canute smiled shyly. 'I'm sorry I didn't tell you before. I know now that I could have, but I'm used to hiding it in my village. When I first found out I could change, I was too young to control it, so a few people found out back then. My parents persuaded them to keep it a secret, but the villagers who knew treated me differently. They said that only Loki, the trickster god, could shapeshift and it was a sign that I couldn't be trusted. That's why I don't have my arm cuff yet,' he added sadly. 'My Jarl is one of the people who know. He agreed that if I won this contest, if I used the magic to remove the dragon inside me, he would finally grant me my arm cuff.'

'That's terrible!' Saga exploded. 'You shouldn't have to change who you are to earn somebody's trust.'

Canute shrugged. 'I didn't know what else to do. My parents were against me coming here, but they didn't try to stop me either, so they must think it's for the best, too.'

'Well, *we* trust you,' Ruvsá said firmly. Saga nodded so hard half of her soup slid out of her bowl. 'And we like you for *you*, which your dragon is a part of.' She dragged in a long breath. 'I didn't tell my parents or brothers I was entering – I just left them a message. I know I wanted to come here to prove that I'm just as good as my brothers, but my family have always celebrated what makes me special. I can communicate with animals,' she admitted to Canute, who looked impressed. Saga was proud on Ruvsá's behalf. 'It's a part of me and I'd never want to get rid of it,' Ruvsá added. 'If I could turn into a dragon, they'd celebrate that too.' Her smile turned mischievous. 'Though it would be great fun to breathe some fire their way, just to give them a little scare.'

'I'll think about keeping my dragon-self,' Canute said, his smile wide and free. He looked the happiest Saga had ever seen him now that he wasn't dragging a heavy secret around. She chewed on her lip, wondering if she should tell him and Ruvsá about the prophecy, how the seers foretold that she held the future of the North in her hands. Before she could decide, some raiders boarded the sledge. Their furs waterlogged and their hair bedraggled, they headed straight for the crackling fire to dry off, drinking bowls of soup to warm their insides. But more than one looked furious.

'Let it go, Knut,' Fenrir said as a raider with the sides of his head shaved glared at Canute and Saga. Knut threw his bow and arrows in their direction, and they clattered loudly, making the children jump.

'It isn't right, Fenrir,' Knut growled. 'These children have strange and unnatural powers, the likes of which I've never seen before. They shouldn't be allowed to use them like this; it isn't fair to the rest of us.' He focused on Canute. 'Especially him, spawn of Loki.'

'Easy.' Fenrir jerked his head at the cauldron of soup. 'Have a hot meal before you leave for the mainland. Put some fire in your belly and you'll soon catch up with Magnus and Vidar. They'll be waiting in the caves half a day's walk from the castle.' Knut nodded, but didn't tear his eyes from Canute. 'Walk away,' Fenrir told him, his voice scraping harsher. 'They're just children.'

'No child of mine ever acted like that,' Knut growled.

'Just because you don't understand something doesn't mean it's unnatural,' Saga said hotly, folding her arms.

'Magic like that shouldn't exist!' Knut pointed angrily at Canute. 'I'm sure the sorcerers would be mighty interested to learn how you have it.'

This was turning out to be a very long day and Saga was frustrated – with the sorcerers, with worrying about where Afi and Dag were and what was happening to them, with battling her fear of magic, then having to deal with everyone's reactions when she finally showed some of the power the seers had foreseen. With Knut's meanness piled on top, it all came crashing down, making Saga finally snap.

'Are you threatening us?' She stood up, clenching her fists.

Knut reared back, terror spreading over his face.

'What?' Saga began, horrified that he seemed to be afraid of her. It was too late. Knut had already begun casting a quick rune that fired its magic at Saga, snapping her arms and legs down as if invisible ropes had fastened round her. She struggled against them, but couldn't open her mouth to speak.

Ruvsá and Canute leaped up at once. 'Undo the binding rune now.' Ruvsá's voice turned deeper as she raised her arms to the skies, suddenly loud and protective. 'Or I shall unleash the vengeance of the skies upon you.'

Above, came the piercing call of a bird of prey, then another and another. It sounded as if she'd called at least a hundred to her aid.

Scales began to ripple over Canute's hands.

Knut's eyes swivelled wildly between them, suddenly realizing that Ruvsá was as powerful as Canute. His fear grew.

Fenrir held his hands up. 'Just calm down,' he told them all, his bushy grey beard twitching anxiously. 'This doesn't need to go any further –'

Saga's shield shimmered to life, breaking the invisible ropes and calling her own magic to the surface. It rose like a storm tide, and when it crashed out of her, Saga could no more hold it back than she could hold back the waves.

Saga's light-bear came hurtling out. It was bigger than it had been in the sea and as it lolloped over to the terrified Knut, she realized that she couldn't control it at all. It paused in front of Knut, opened its jaws to reveal huge teeth, each one a spear of pure light, and roared. Its roar was a soundless, sparkling river of light and power. It shook the entire sledge with its might. Even Holger, who had remained indifferent to the unspooling fight, was braced with an ice crystal in each hand.

But Knut had received the light-bear's attack in full. It barrelled into him, sending him flying out of the sledge and skidding over the snow.

There was a long silence as everyone looked warily at Saga and her light-bear. Saga suddenly felt drained, as if all her bones had melted together and there was nothing left to make her stand up. She slumped down, exhausted, the light-bear winking out of sight the moment she hit the floor.

'She just needs rest,' she heard Canute saying as Ruvsá held her hand tightly.

But there were other voices making themselves heard too. As the rest of the contestants and Rollo boarded the sledge, dragging Knut along with them, those voices grew louder.

'She clearly cannot control her magic,' one of the shieldmaidens declared.

'She's dangerous and a threat to us all,' a storyteller, who had travelled to the Far North by himself, announced.

Saga felt as if she'd sprouted a second head the way everyone kept glancing furtively at her. Her eyelids drooped. That huge rush of magic had taken its toll and she wished they didn't have to journey across the vast snowy expanse to return to the castle. She wished that she was already curling up in her furs with Bjørn's warmth pressed against her.

As the sorcerers discarded more ice crystals, now spent and dull, to lift the sledge up from the snow and begin its flight home, sleep rushed over Saga like a blanket being pulled over her head.

CHAPTER TWENTY-THREE
THE STORM

When Saga awoke, the mood inside the sledge was as thick as pack ice and impossible to cut through. There were only around fifteen contestants now. They'd lost another handful, thankfully including Knut, who must have been sent off the sledge while she was sleeping. She sat up and her head rushed.

'Steady.' Ruvsá held on to her until she regained her balance and the sky and floor were in the right places again.

They were approaching the ice castle. A thousand stars glistened above it and the Northern Lights flickered through the sky. Now and then, they danced through Bifrost and the rainbow bridge of light turned incandescent. Saga wondered what it would sound like if you stood on it – if its magical hum would be an exquisite melody or a deafening roar; if its light would be beautiful or too dazzling for mortal eyes.

Sorcerers stood at the tip of the treacherous mountain of ice, high above the tallest castle turret, harvesting the Lights. They presented an ethereal image as the Lights ebbed and flowed around them, and for a moment Saga wondered if they were truly human. They seemed like the gods, who didn't really care what people did as long as it didn't affect them.

She was still muddling through it when they hopped up the ice flume, returning to another great feast laid out in the frosted hall. This time, the second table had been removed; most of the fifty contestants had left now. As ever, it was dark. Saga felt the disorientating twist of time, not knowing whether this was breakfast or the evening meal. Either way, the remaining contestants fell on it as if they'd never seen food before, and Saga's stomach snarled at the sight of it all.

Canute laughed at her. 'That always happens when I've turned into a dragon. My father likes to joke that I have the appetite of a dragon as well.'

Saga gave him an exhausted smile before she went to her room. When she returned with Bjørn, he growled at Canute again, sensing the scales under his skin, the dragon slumbering inside the boy. But this time Saga was prepared for it and she stroked Bjørn as Ruvsá softly sang to him in her language, of the dragon that was a friend and a bear that had nothing to fear. When Bjørn calmed, the three of them helped themselves to the biggest plates they could find and began the process of adding everything to them. Fire-baked breads that they softened in hot, flavourful bowls of reindeer stew, roasted aurochs of which Bjørn devoured more than his fair share, platters of crispy vegetables strewn with herbs, salted fish and a creamy mushroom soup that Saga particularly liked, although she picked out the chunks of mushrooms, explaining to Ruvsá, 'I like the taste of them. I just don't like their bodies – they're too . . . slimy.'

The raiders and shieldmaidens kept their distance from the children, though their gaze fell in their direction more than once. Bjørn growled softly, staying closer than usual to Saga, his fur pressed against her back as he guarded her. Even the sorcerers were keeping watch. Saga hated that they all knew that she couldn't control her magic. Worse, that some of them were afraid of her, but she didn't blame them; she'd terrified herself. The biggest disappointment was Torben, who hadn't spoken to her once since her light-bear had thrown Knut out of the sledge. He wasn't even close to Knut – Saga had never seen them talk that much to each other – but Torben seemed as wary as the other raiders of her wild magic. Only Unn and Leif were indifferent and had sat near the children.

'What happened back there?' Ruvsá asked.

'I couldn't control it,' Saga sighed. 'It just came out of nowhere and stormed through me and I didn't understand what was happening or how to make it stop. It felt like my body didn't belong to me any more.' The worst thing was now that she knew she was powerful, she didn't know how to use that power to find Afi and Dag, or if she could even control it enough to fight off a mountain troll, let alone a whole *tribe* of trolls.

Bjørn gave a low whine and nudged an entire cake over to Saga with his nose. She smiled and cut herself a generous slice.

Canute pulled a strange expression.

'What?' Saga asked.

'I know how you feel,' he said.

'Then why are you making that face?'

Now Canute looked puzzled. 'What face?'

Ruvsá gestured at him with a chunk of bread. 'I think that was his sympathetic face,' she added helpfully.

'Anyway,' Canute said, his ears turning pink, 'when I first discovered that I could turn into a dragon, I couldn't control it either. My sister would borrow my skates without asking and lose them, and, next thing I knew, I'd have scales and horns and a tail.'

'Once I was so cross with my older brothers that I accidentally made the whole reindeer herd chase them. They had to climb up a tree to get away from their antlers.' Ruvsá laughed. 'It's just practice. And we can help with that.'

Saga chased the last crumbs of cake around the plate with her finger. 'But my parents were the best rune-casters my village had seen in generations and they couldn't control their magic. When the trolls came the first time, my parents' magic was too powerful and it killed the trolls, but also my mother and father.' She touched her silver hair, the reminder of how her parents' deaths had marked her. 'What if I accidentally use too much and it drains my life-force too? If my parents couldn't control their magic, I don't have any hope of controlling mine!'

'What did your afi say about it?' Ruvsá asked curiously. 'You're always talking about his stories. He must have told you something?'

Saga fidgeted. 'He told me that they had full command over their magic, that they chose to sacrifice themselves to protect me.' Suddenly she didn't feel hungry any more, just tired. 'That the only thing that was ever out of their control was how much they loved me. But now they're gone and I can never ask them if that was true or show them how much I love them back.'

'You can show them your love by honouring them with your magic,' Ruvsá told her. 'You're a part of them and they will always be with you. Look how your shield refuses to leave you – that's because their love will never end.'

Saga buried her face in Bjørn's fur, her eyes watering. He snuffled at her hair. 'I'm fine,' she croaked. 'Let's talk about something else now.'

The gods granted her wish.

Vigga, the oldest sorcerer they'd seen so far, came rushing into the great hall as fast as she could, her ice crystal bobbing on her forehead, her robes and sparse silver hair windswept. Some of the sorcerers stood at once and a deep silence spread through the hall.

'A terrible storm is rolling in over the horizon,' Vigga gasped, leaning on the sorcerers' table to catch her breath. 'One that I fear has been sent by the gods to test us. If we do not secure the castle . . .'

Alarm stirred through the sorcerers. Saga noticed that Rollo continued to eat calmly.

'Why are they worried?' Canute whispered to her and Ruvsá. 'The whole castle is magical!'

Holger stood. The runes on his cheeks dappled as he spoke: 'Contestants, return to your rooms. The third and final challenge is cancelled until further notice.' He pivoted to address the sorcerers. 'Sorcerers, take up your assigned positions to raise the shields.'

There was a growing murmur of concern mixed with frustration. Solveig stalked from the room with an entire cake under her arm, followed by the rest of the shieldmaidens. The raiders exited quickly after them, taking their horns of mead with them. Leif looked more squirrelly than usual as he waited for Unn.

Unn turned to the children. 'Do not be frightened,' she said kindly, tucking a strand of red hair behind her ear. 'You can wait out the storm with us, if you like?'

Saga stared at her. Canute paused in stuffing his pockets with biscuits. They'd voyaged to the Far North, climbed into a white-bear den and dived into the depths of the icy ocean – one little storm wasn't going to scare them now!

'That's very kind of you, but we'll be fine,' Ruvsá said quickly. Saga, Bjørn and Canute followed Ruvsá out of the great hall. Before they entered the icy passageway that led to their rooms, Saga glanced back in time to see Rollo use several ice crystals to conjure a huge, glimmering shield of magic that rippled out, covering the windows and stretching to where she couldn't see its limits. It was darker than her parents' shield had been, thicker and purple-tinted, but it still plunged Saga back to being five years old and, with a dizzying whirl, she suddenly remembered that day again, as clearly as the smoothest waters.

Falling against the thick ice wall, Saga was barely aware of Bjørn's alarmed yowl as he rushed to her side, holding her up, Ruvsá and Canute running back to her. All she could see was that moment when her mother and father had looked at her, hiding under the table, then at each other, their hands linked tightly. Saga's mother had yanked the single ice crystal she'd been wearing round her neck and, as one, they cast the shield that exploded their longhouse with its magical force.

'My mother *did* use her ice crystal,' Saga whispered to her bear and her friends, all crowded around her. 'That means I was worried about using normal runes for nothing. It wasn't using runes that killed them . . . It was an ice crystal.' She looked up at her friends, searching their faces for answers. 'But where did these new runes come from? What if they're more dangerous?'

'The only thing that's dangerous is your fear.' Ruvsá rubbed Saga's back as if she was soothing a wild animal. 'It makes you panic and you lose control over your magic, and that's when things go wrong. But it doesn't have to be like that.'

Saga nodded. 'I know I need to practise.' She sniffed and wiped her eyes with her sleeve. Bjørn whined sadly and shuffled even closer, stroking her with one careful paw. 'If I'd been practising all along, I could have rescued Afi by myself in the first place!'

Canute shook his head. 'You're powerful, Saga, but you're not take-on-a-whole-tribe-of-trolls-by-yourself powerful. Anyway, didn't the seer tell you to enter the contest? They know everything – she wouldn't have said that if you didn't need to be here.'

Saga let her friends help her up, their expressions kind. But, as they made their way back to their rooms, she couldn't stop wondering. Why *did* she need to be here? What more did the seer know?

That night, Saga hugged Bjørn extra tight. He gave an inquisitive huff and placed a paw on her back. 'I wielded magic today, Bjørn,' Saga whispered into his fur. 'Real, powerful magic. And it was a rune I'd only seen in my dreams. What can that mean?' She remembered the seer's prophecy as if it was written on her skin. She repeated it now: ' "She will dream magic," the prophecy said. This must be what they meant.' But now, as the storm laid siege to the ice castle and Ruvsá was lost in sleep, a deep chill descended on Saga. *Fear*. 'What about the second part of the prophecy?' Bjørn whined softly and rested another paw on her head. Its weight soothed Saga though her thoughts still flurried like a snowstorm. This was the part that troubled her the most, the part she had not shared with Ruvsá and Canute in case it shattered their newfound friendship. ' "She will hold the fate of the North in her hands." What can that mean?' Saga frowned in the dark. Could rescuing her village have some bigger effect than being reunited with Afi and Dag? 'And what if all this was a colossal mistake?

We've wasted so much time here and I need to get to Afi. Maybe we should just leave?' Bjørn huffed. 'You're right, the seer told me to come here to save them. Ugh!' She didn't know what the right decision was and couldn't stop panicking that either way she'd choose the wrong thing to do and end up losing the most precious things in the world to her. Saga groaned and flopped down on her furs, waiting for sleep to reach out with its creeping fingers and steal her away. She was more tired than she'd ever been, so she closed her eyes and waited.

But sleep did not come. The more Saga tried to sleep, the more her thoughts and fears swirled about in her head until she found herself getting up, pulling on her boots and softly opening the door. It creaked on its frosted hinges and Saga stopped, but Ruvsá only turned on her side, muttering to herself in her dreams.

Saga slipped out of their room.

Bjørn padded after her on silent paws. Hunter's paws. Since Saga's legs were still aching from her icy plunge after the whale tusk, she pulled herself on to his back.

'Let's go to the hot springs,' she whispered.

Out in the passageway, a roar battered the magical shields and the ice creaked and shifted around them.

'Wait.' Saga laid a warning hand on Bjørn's shoulders. 'Rollo was in the great hall. Maybe we should go to the storage cave instead of the hot springs? I bet we could find you something tasty to eat down there. What do you think?'

Bjørn snapped his jaws together with excitement and Saga stifled a giggle. They set off together. Down one twisting passageway and up the next. Other than the crunch of Bjørn's claws on the ice and the storm raging on, it was silent. The contestants were all in their rooms, the sorcerers otherwise occupied. The blue-green lanternlight cast eerie shadows on the frozen walls, and the carved runes shimmered like pale moonlight as they passed.

'We should be there by now,' Saga said out loud, her voice echoing in the darkness as it slowly dawned on her that they were lost somewhere deep inside the forbidden castle.

CHAPTER TWENTY-FOUR
LOST IN THE ICE CASTLE

'We need to find the way back to our room,' Saga whispered to Bjørn. She was beginning to panic. If the sorcerers caught them roaming the forbidden halls of their mountain castle, then she would be thrown out of the contest faster than Thor could toss a lightning bolt across the sky.

They darted through another huge hall, dripping with icicles and silence. Large silver scorch marks spun out from the centre and Bjørn carefully avoided stepping on them with his paws. 'Someone must have wielded powerful magic here.' Saga shivered and they hurried on through a narrow passageway that forced Saga to duck, and into a room that she thought was small until she looked up and her head swirled. It was taller than five trees, with one long shelf carved out of the ice that spiralled all the way up, holding hundreds of stone tablets, carved with runes. 'A library of magic,' Saga said wonderingly before they quickly left to try another passageway.

Outside, the storm howled louder, the magical shields whining with effort as powerful winds swooped down from the mountaintop to shake the castle walls. It reminded Saga how far north they were, how the castle stuck out of the snowy plain like a shard of ice, on an island surrounded by deep, cold water. She couldn't stop picturing a giant wave rolling out of the sea and rushing over the snow, smashing into the ice castle and sending it toppling. Watery fingers claiming its shattered remains and dragging them down to the same dark depths into which she'd plunged to find that whale tusk. And deeper still.

'We really need to go back now,' Saga told Bjørn, hoping that the passageway they were hurrying down led somewhere either of them recognized.

It did not. Instead, it yawned open into another cavernous room, one that strangely held no lanterns or sconces. It had been left in the dark. Frowning, Saga dived deep into the last shred of energy she had to draw the smallest rune. She was scared that conjuring the light-bear again would be a huge mistake, but she was too curious to learn what the sorcerers hadn't wanted anyone to see to play it safe. She didn't trust them and now that she was already lost, she might as well do some snooping. A miniature light-bear appeared on the palm of her hand. Saga sighed in relief. It sparkled brighter than an ice crystal, creating a pool of light that surrounded Saga and her bear. Bjørn turned his head to watch the light-bear prowl along Saga's fingers. She lifted her hand high, turning her attention to the room.

And nearly dropped her little light-bear.

Pictures were painted on the ice walls. Saga slid from Bjørn's back to take a closer look. Her tiny light-bear soared up, dancing along the wall, making the pictures glow. They told stories of the sorcerers and how they came to be the guardians of Bifrost. They told of a time long ago, lost to human memory but preserved in ancient ice, when the first sorcerers had aided the gods in their worlds-shaking battle against the frost giants. When the gods finally banished the frost giants to their frozen realm of Jötunheimr, and returned home to Asgard, they left the bridge between the human realm and Asgard, the realm of the gods, under the protection of the sorcerers.

'Well, the human side of it, that is,' Saga said out loud, running her hand over the picture of the burning bridge, guarded by robed sorcerers on one end, and the all-seeing god, Heimdall, on the Asgardian side. 'But I don't understand.' She turned back to her bear. 'Why hide this in darkness? This is the sorcerers' legacy ... There's something strange going on in this castle, Bjørn,' she said suspiciously. 'I can feel it gnawing at my bones. Something just doesn't make sense to me, but I can't figure out what or why.'

Bjørn whined sympathetically. Saga clambered up on to his back, letting her light-bear fade away as they exited the hall of stories and headed down another passageway. She sniffed and rubbed her sleeve against her nose.

'It's growing colder,' she said, hunkering deeper down inside her furs, glad she'd brought them. 'We must be far from the core of the ice castle now.' It was warmest in the great hall, where there was only a thin layer of magic protecting the huge windows cut from the ice, leaving the hall bare to passing clouds and snowdrifts. Bjørn padded along faster, but Saga didn't know which direction to take next. They were still lost.

Suddenly, they turned a corner and heard something.

Bjørn halted and Saga held her breath, the pair listening as one. There came the faint sound of metal clanging rhythmically. Saga tried to work out what it could be when the answer came rushing to her. It was the same sound she'd heard all over the castle when it grew silent: the distant hammering of picks against thick ice. 'They're mining ice crystals down there,' she realized.

'We must be close to an entrance to the mines.' This was chased by the sinking knowledge that they were more lost than she'd thought. Saga hesitated, listening harder, curious about the sorcerers who toiled down there – it sounded as if there were hundreds. How many sorcerers lived in this great ice castle? And why did she never see the ones who mined at mealtimes? There was so much about the sorcerers that she didn't understand and now that she'd had a little taste of their world she was hungry to know more.

Bjørn huffed and made to turn away, but Saga whispered, 'Stop.' She chewed her lip for a moment. She was already in danger of being caught and banished from the contest – she should have gone running back to her room and crept under her bundle of furs as fast as she could – but Saga had never been a girl who'd done as she was told.

'Let's go and have a quick look,' she finally decided. Bjørn growled a warning. 'Just one tiny peek,' Saga promised, and Bjørn relented, ambling further towards the mines.

The sound of hammering and chiselling grew louder, the frozen passageways becoming narrower and colder until it was so cold that Saga couldn't feel her fingers and her breath looked like dragon smoke. When the passageway veered sharply to the left, Bjørn had to squeeze himself through, grumbling at the tight fit. It widened back out, but it was darker here and Saga couldn't stop her teeth chattering.

In front of them stood a door.

Saga's breath trembled in her lungs. She climbed off Bjørn, who nipped at her furs, trying to stop her, and hesitated, looking at the door. Unlike the rest of the castle's doors, which were ice or iron, this one was carved from a single piece of ancient wood, and scarred with old runes, so many that they overlapped into a single, unreadable pattern. Saga was standing at the beating heart of the ice castle. Reaching her hand out slowly, she was about to touch the iron handle when she snapped her hand back, feeling guilty. She couldn't tell what might happen if she tried to open this door. And she had to stay in the contest if she wanted to save Afi and Dag – what was she doing risking everything like this? 'Let's go and find our room now.' She cast one last curious look back at the door before holding on to Bjørn's fur, ready to hop up on to his back.

Before she could move, she heard voices coming down the passageway. Luckily, it bent and curved like a river, so Saga hadn't been spotted yet.

'Sorcerers!' she hissed, looking for somewhere to hide.

'I suspect Rollo,' Vigga's old voice creaked out.

Saga hesitated, one hand on her bear.

'You think he conjured this storm?' Holger's voice mused. 'For what purpose?'

'A distraction,' Vigga continued, 'so that while we busy ourselves bracing the castle against the wrath of his magic, he can steal away to Bifrost.'

Saga's mouth fell open.

'Then we must hasten up to the peak at once,' Holger interrupted.

Vigga made a strange noise that sounded as if she had a bone stuck in her throat. It took Saga a moment to realize that she was laughing. 'Oh, Holger, you forget how much older I am than I look,' she chortled. 'I am sending a guard up there, one that will prove to be more than Rollo can handle by himself.'

Their voices were coming closer, their footsteps nearing. In a panic, Saga whirled round, wondering if they could make it to the end of the passageway in time, but it stretched out longer than she'd remembered. A crunch of ice signalled that the sorcerers were almost upon them. Another heartbeat and they'd round the bend and see Saga.

Her heart thudding, Saga ran over to the door to the mines and wrenched it open. Bjørn silently skidded inside and she fled after him, shutting the door behind them both.

CHAPTER TWENTY-FIVE
THE SECRET OF THE MINES

Saga turned round.

At her feet, the ice dropped away into a sheer staircase. Unlike the others dotted around the sprawling castle, this one was narrow and dark. The ice walls were uneven here too, with chunks of rock and grey veins bulging out. It smelled fusty, as if it had forgotten what fresh air was, and it was cold. Terribly cold. Saga held on to Bjørn tightly so that they could keep each other warm. He snuffled grumpily at her.

'I know,' Saga groaned. 'I'm sorry! But we had to hide from the sorcerers. Anyway, now that we're here, maybe we should have a quick look? The sorcerers could be coming in here any moment and I don't want to be standing behind the door if they open it!'

Bjørn lowered his head and shoulders, letting Saga climb on to his back.

Together, they descended into the mines.

Green flames suddenly whooshed up the walls. The ice-rock stairway glittered eerily and as Bjørn slowly walked down the carved ice steps, digging his claws in so that they wouldn't slip, Saga gazed at the walls. They were studded with iridescent ice crystals that flashed and twinkled green from the flames. The sound of tinkering steadily grew louder as Bjørn continued to clamber down the steps and Saga's nerves swelled.

'What do you think it looks like?' she whispered, imagining lots of dark caves, sparkling with crystals, that sorcerers crawled through, prising their magical treasure out of the rock and ice. She wondered if this was how her afi had felt when he'd gone into the elves' smithy in search of a red-gold weapon that would make his enemies shiver in their boots. A hard lump settled in Saga's throat and she clung tighter to Bjørn. She missed home. She'd never been away from it for this long before, nor this far, and she'd give anything to be back there right now, snuggled by the fire with Bjørn curled round her, listening to one of her afi's stories. As if she'd conjured it, her afi's voice rang through her head: 'You were named Saga after the great stories that shaped our history and the ones still to come. But you, little Saga, are my favourite story of all.'

Saga tried not to sniffle.

Bjørn stilled. Saga hadn't noticed the stairway had finally come to an end. It took a moment for her eyes to adjust to the deep gloom. The darkness was as thick as the storm clouds that had descended on the castle, lit by flashes as the pickaxes sparked against rock. Something prickled at Saga. Something wasn't right here – she could feel it.

Before them was a viewing platform with a single lantern clamped to its iron railing. Saga held tighter on to Bjørn as he slowly prowled towards it, his hunter's instincts as sharp as his claws. The lantern's green-blue light flickered in and out as the ice crystal mounted at its core struggled along, its magic weak. It needed taking up to the tip of the mountain peak where the Northern Lights shone down and the sorcerers stole rays of its light to fill the gemstones with magic. But she'd seen the sorcerers discard ice crystals instead of refilling them, suggesting that they had more than plenty – so why were they putting up with lanterns failing down in the mines? Bjørn drew alongside the lantern and there, with one bright pulse of its remaining magic, a shaft of green-blue light beamed out across a huge open pit below and Saga suddenly saw the truth.

There were no sorcerers in the mines.

There were villagers.

More people than Saga had ever met in her life filled the main pit of the mine, chiselling through the walls until they tunnelled out into a warren of caves. Hundreds of ice crystals sparkled, heaped on top of sledges that people towed away with ropes, moving them to another location Saga couldn't see. Enough ice crystals for the sorcerers to harvest more magic than Saga could imagine existing. Enough to take over the land from sea to sea and worse, deplete the Northern Lights of their magic until they blinked out of existence. Saga struggled to breathe at the enormity of what this all meant.

'This is their secret,' she whispered to Bjørn. 'What are we going to do now?'

His fur rose.

Heavy footfalls stomped into the pit. The villagers huddled closer together, wielding their pickaxes harder as the ice and rock shuddered beneath their feet. Bjørn retreated into the shadows with Saga still on his back. When she peered down to see what was happening, another realization came hurtling at her like a lightning bolt.

It was a mountain troll.

'The village raids,' she gasped. 'The mountain trolls are bringing the villagers *here*?'

The troll dragged its tree-club through the pit, its two heads swivelling around to keep all four eyes on the villagers. It wore a wolfskin cloak and mushrooms sprouted from inside its ears. It stopped to snarl at someone.

Saga leaned forward to see better, searching through the huddles of villagers, though she hoped she was wrong and that she wouldn't see –

'*Afi*,' Saga breathed. He looked older than when she'd last seen him, his back beginning to bend, his grey beard dull and straggly. Next to him was Dag and a couple of other villagers Saga recognized. All of them looked dirty and exhausted. Saga tried to climb off Bjørn, but he backed into the rock to stop her.

'Let me down!' She struggled. 'I have to get to them. I have to. Afi!' she shouted across the pit.

He looked up.

With a jolt, their eyes met. Seeing that familiar glacial blue rocked Saga to her core. Even at a distance, she saw worry and fear flit through her afi. Dag's mouth fell open and he stepped forward, but Afi held him back, shaking his head in warning.

The mountain troll raised its heads, hunting for the source of the disturbance, but before it could set its eyes on Saga, Bjørn lashed a paw out, knocking the lantern off its hook.

It shattered, the light winking out.

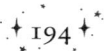

Some villagers screamed as they were plunged into blackness, but Saga didn't have enough breath in her lungs to scream. Frozen air was whipping past her face as Bjørn ran. Faster and faster, he ran back to the staircase and up the ice steps until they'd reached the wooden door at the top.

Saga was too shocked to move or open it, but Bjørn refused to slow and they barrelled through it, forcing the door open and sliding back on to the lower floor of the castle. The door slammed shut behind them. They both panted for a moment, catching their breath, listening for any signs that sorcerers were roaming nearby. Or that the mountain troll had chased them up the stairs.

And then something peculiar happened.

Saga, who had lived with fear as her constant shadow, was no longer afraid. Discovering that her afi was the sorcerers' prisoner had ignited a spark of rage that burned brightly inside her ribcage. She clenched her fists. She was going to nurture that spark until it grew strong enough to set the whole ice castle alight.

PART THREE
THE UPRISING

*She felt like the cry of war before a battle, the
spark on a stone that grows a flame.*

CHAPTER TWENTY-SIX
SAGA'S DISCOVERY

Bjørn hurtled back through the ice castle as if he was determined to return Saga to their room before she could make any more dangerous decisions. It was all Saga could do to cling tightly to his fur, half frozen with shock.

Just as they reached the main hall, its tables empty and awaiting the breakfast feast, Saga realized they were no longer alone. A sorcerer was standing with his back to them, his long silver hair and narrow shoulders instantly recognizable: it was Rollo. He had returned to his post since Saga had overheard Vigga and the other sorcerer discussing him, and was holding an ice crystal in one hand, thickening the magical shield that the storm screamed and tore at.

Bjørn dug his claws into the ice, stopping so fast that Saga toppled off his back.

'Why are you in such a hurry?' Rollo arched one thin silver eyebrow as he stared down at Saga, his pinched face tighter than usual. 'Could it be because you know well that all contestants are forbidden from roaming the halls of our ice castle? You entered from another direction to the hot springs or the rooms.' He bent closer, his lip curling. 'Are you truly breaking our laws?'

Saga felt as if all the air had been sucked from the hall. As if she'd been plunged back into the sea of ice and whales. 'I-I –' She swallowed. Bjørn growled and Saga's hand tightened on his fur as she stood. 'I didn't mean to,' she finished weakly, unable to forage for a better lie. She could not be sent away now. Not now that she had finally found her afi, who had turned out to be *right here*, within the castle itself.

Rollo ignored Bjørn, fixing his pale stare more intently on Saga. 'You are fortunate that it is in my own interests that you are not removed from the contest. Go now and never let me catch you again.'

Saga bit her lip hard enough to taste rust. She should have run away the moment he told her to go, but she couldn't help asking, needing to know, 'Why is it in your best interests that I stay?' She met his stare, wondering if he knew about the villagers down in the mines and the mountain trolls that had snatched them away to this island. Surely he did – from what she'd overheard Vigga saying, it seemed that Rollo had a secret, terrible agenda of his own. One that involved Bifrost. She swallowed nervously. This was a sorcerer who dared to threaten the gods themselves – she was far out of her depth here.

Rollo straightened. He removed a speck of snow from his blue cloak. 'I happen to have made a wager that you shall win the contest. A large wager.' His grey eyes glittered. 'Do not disappoint me now,' he said icily.

Saga was stunned. This was the last thing she'd expected him to say, and she didn't understand what this could mean. Although if someone like Rollo believed she could win the contest . . . Bjørn nipped her hand.

Saga recalled herself in a hurry. 'I won't,' she said with fresh determination before climbing again on to Bjørn's back and riding her bear away. When she glanced behind them, the great hall was empty once more.

'Ruvsá. Wake up.'

Ruvsá sat up, blinking fiercely. 'Is it morning?' she asked, her breath misting around her furs. Their fire had burned low, dwindling to glowing embers, as all the sorcerers' attention and magic had been redirected to the storm.

Saga shook her head. 'It is night still. Oh, Ruvsá, I've found something so terrible I don't know what to do.' The image of her afi working in the mine haunted Saga. She kept seeing his hollowed-out face, his starving eyes. Saga shivered.

'Get in.' Ruvsá held out her furs and Saga slid inside. The last time she'd huddled together with someone for warmth she had been with Dag, when they'd got lost sailing through the fjord in a snowstorm. They'd pulled Saga's little longboat up on a rocky outcrop and turned it upside down to shelter beneath, next to Bjørn. Dag had worried that the snow would cover the boat and themselves, leaving nothing for anyone to find by the time a search party came. But Saga had kept peering outside, knowing that her afi would come for her sooner than that. And he had. Striding through the storm with his glacier-blue eyes burning brightly as he searched through the snow for her. Now Saga smouldered with anger at the thought of her proud, strong afi being forced to work in the mines, at the thought of his eyes, once bright with spirit, now dimmed. With a trembling voice, Saga told Ruvsá what she had discovered.

When she had finished, Ruvsá fetched Canute. After he'd cast a basic rune to light another fire, Saga told the story for the second time. This time, her voice did not shake or shiver. This time, it turned fierce, because Saga would not let anyone make a prisoner of her afi. And she told Ruvsá and Canute so.

'Wait a moment before you go rushing off on some heroic quest,' Ruvsá told her. 'You said that you saw entire villages of people working down there?'

Saga nodded.

'Where were the rest of the trolls?' Ruvsá asked.

'I don't know. I only saw one. But what does that matter?' Saga's impatience was swelling. 'We have a dragon!'

Canute spluttered. 'I'm not battling against an entire tribe of mountain trolls!'

Saga sighed, starting to pace. She tugged at her hair. 'There's one thing I can't figure out, though.'

'What?' Ruvsá watched her walk back and forth as she warmed her hands on the fire.

Saga held up one finger. 'First, we have the mountain trolls and villagers down in the mines.' She held up a second finger on her other hand. 'Then, we have the conversation I overheard about Rollo creating the storm as a distraction so that he could sneak away to Bifrost for some reason we all think is bad, but we don't know for sure.'

'So?' Canute looked at her.

'So –' Saga drew her two fingers together – 'are these both related to some huge thing that's going on inside the castle, or –' she drew them apart again – 'are they two different things that are just happening at the same time?'

'And, if they are related, how many of the sorcerers are in on it?' Ruvsá added grimly. 'Because we might not be battling against just the mountain trolls – it could be the entire ice castle as well.'

Saga stopped pacing.

Canute looked horrified. 'If it's the entire ice castle as well as the trolls, we don't stand a chance. There are hundreds of sorcerers with more powerful magic than ours.'

'They have more than magic,' Ruvsá continued as Saga and Canute both looked at her. 'They have a plan. And if we're going to try to go up against them, we need to have a plan too. Canute's right – we can't outfight all of them, but we might be able to out*wit* them.'

Saga's impatience waned. 'You'll really help me?'

Ruvsá nodded. 'Of course! You didn't think we'd let you face this by yourself, did you?' Saga had learned by now that Ruvsá's quietness hid a fierce and protective nature, but it still surprised her when it popped out now and then.

'Why are you including me in this?' Canute grumbled.

'Because we're a team. And, more than that, we're friends,' Ruvsá said firmly. 'And friends don't let friends charge into danger alone.'

Canute sighed. 'Fine.'

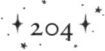

Saga threw her arms round both of them, her friends. 'Thank you,' she mumbled into Ruvsá's hair.

'So, what are we going to do?' Canute's forehead creased with worry when the three of them broke awkwardly apart. Their friendship was new, like freshly formed ice. The edges were still sharp, not yet smoothed, and you had to learn where to step.

Saga smiled. 'I have a plan.'

CHAPTER TWENTY-SEVEN
SAGA'S PLAN

'That is a *terrible* plan,' Canute said.

Saga gave him an indignant look.

'Well, it is!' he protested. 'You were lucky Rollo only caught you in the great hall, not coming out of the mines or, worse, inside the mines. You could have been troll food! And now you want to go back out there?' Canute exchanged a glance with Ruvsá. 'It's a terrible idea. He's probably still there and you won't get away with it twice in one night.'

Ruvsá bit her lip.

'Do you think it's a bad idea as well?' Saga asked her in a quiet voice.

'It's not even a plan, really,' Canute continued as if Saga hadn't spoken. 'It's a plan to make a plan.'

Saga whirled round. 'Do you have a better idea, then?' she demanded.

'Yes,' Canute said. 'We go back to focusing on the contest and when one of us wins that horn of magic ice crystals, we use it to free the villagers. Then we go home. We can tell our Jarls about the sorcerers and then they can investigate anything strange happening up here in the Far North while we sit by the fire, telling stories of how we bested a sledge-load of raiders and warriors to the prize.'

'If you ignore the fact that none of us might win, what would you do after that?' Saga asked. 'When the villagers are free and all the magic is used up and maybe we've defeated the trolls but we're still here, in the ice castle, facing a horde of angry sorcerers? What happens then?'

Canute fell silent.

'The seer told me to come here, to enter the contest – this has to be the reason why!' Saga cried out.

'Knowledge is always useful,' Ruvsá added. 'Saga's right. We can't plan properly if we don't know what the sorcerers are actually doing.'

'Thank you.' Saga sighed in relief.

'But Canute has a good point too,' Ruvsá carried on, ignoring Saga's frown. 'It's too risky to go creeping around the castle for a second time tonight. Especially with all the sorcerers on alert with this storm. Maybe tomorrow night will be better if it's calmed down.'

Saga stood up. 'No. I've journeyed to the Far North, carved my first runes, walked into a white-bear den and plunged deep into the sea for a lost whale tusk. All that time, I've been waiting and worrying about how to find my afi and Dag. Wondering if I was too late, if I was doing all of this for nothing. But I wasn't and now they're *here* and I am not going to let them spend a day longer down there than they have to. Not them nor any of the villagers. And if you won't come with me because you're scared of the sorcerers or being thrown out of the contest, that's fine, but don't ask me to stay.' Ruvsá and Canute were silent after Saga had finished. 'Come on, Bjørn,' she said, grabbing her furs and leaving the room. Ruvsá and Canute didn't follow her. Saga felt their absence like a shard of ice, piercing and cold.

Saga crept along the glittering ice passageway, Bjørn at her back. The night had deepened and she hoped there was enough time left to investigate before another dark day dawned. She tiptoed into the great hall, casting a wary eye about her in case Rollo had reappeared. But he was nowhere to be seen. The storm still laid siege to the thick castle walls, with vicious winds and hail whipping past the windows in a howling haze. If Saga wanted to learn what was happening, she needed to go straight to the heart of the mystery: she needed to discover what Rollo was doing up by Bifrost that Vigga and the other sorcerers were worried about. But that would mean finding a way up to the mountaintop, teetering above the castle in a terrible magical storm.

Just the thought of it was enough to make her knees shake, but if Rollo had done it that meant it wasn't impossible, and there was nothing she wouldn't do to save her afi. That flame inside her burned a little brighter.

Saga peered into a handful of different passageways before she found the route that would take her up, higher than the castle. A ring of ice crystals was embedded in rune-inscribed ice, their light forming a dazzling circle. When Saga looked up, she saw the stars. 'This must be it, then,' she told Bjørn, who pressed close to her side, refusing to let her enter the ring of light by herself. As soon as they reached the centre, Saga felt as if she'd stepped into water. Her weight was supported as the magic gently lifted both her and Bjørn, higher and higher, until her ears popped, and they emerged at the top.

They were left standing on the great frozen peak of the mountain, high above the ice castle, where the storm was demonstrating its full power. Saga clung on to Bjørn before the wind stole her off the mountain. Hail hammered into her, she was soaked wet already, and she didn't dare move in case she fell. She only hoped that venturing up here might help her figure out what was happening in the castle and its mines – if Vigga had left it guarded from Rollo, there must be *something* important up here, and she needed to find out what.

'The guard.' Saga panicked. 'Bjørn, I forgot about the guard!' She couldn't see anyone up on the mountaintop. There was too much thick grey haze and ice hurtling down into her face. The storm was like a pack of ghosts that had descended on the castle in attack, and no lantern could cut through the gloom. But . . . *there*. A flash of light and colour. It was too stormy for the Northern Lights to appear on a night – or day – like this, but beyond the highest peak of the mountain was a sliver of air with a fatal drop. And, beyond that, the twinkling first step of Bifrost, the shimmering rainbow bridge that led to other worlds. Saga stared at it, moving forward as if she was drawn to it, but Bjørn growled a warning and caught the back of her furs in his teeth, drawing her away from the edge and to safety. As he did, Saga squinted through the storm, desperate to peek at the bridge, to see if she could catch a glimpse of another world.

Then she spotted something else.

She and Bjørn were not the only ones on the mountaintop; a lone sorcerer stood on the peak.

Saga couldn't make out who it was, but they were right on the edge, facing Bifrost, their blue cloak snapping in the storm.

'Is that the guard?' she wondered aloud. 'Or is that Rollo and has he got past the guard? Oh, I wish the others were here. Maybe they'd know what to do!' She sucked in a breath, curious to see whether the sorcerer was going to try to step on to Bifrost, and what might happen if they did, until she focused on the bridge itself. It was burning bright with light and, even through the ferocious weather, a glimpse of it was dazzling. As her eyes adjusted, she spotted a second figure, standing on Bifrost itself.

Saga gasped. The sorcerer was speaking to someone from another world. Nobody else could have stood on that burning bridge without consequences.

'I was right,' she told Bjørn over the screaming wind. He growled his agreement. 'Something strange *is* going on here. We need to hear what they're saying. Maybe if I –' She yanked off a mitten. At once, the bitter temperatures seized her hand, turning it red and numb, but she ignored that, reaching down to the snow piled around her boots and inscribing a rune: a few short lines that looked like two mountains on their sides, their peaks meeting. Dagaz: the moment when light breaks through darkness and understanding clears a murky head. Saga shoved her hand back into her mitten. It was stiff and she couldn't feel her little finger any more, but she couldn't think about that now. She needed her rune to work. She stared at it, willing it to hum to life and make her understand what was happening. *Nothing.*

Just when Saga was about to give up on her rune, it gave a dull twinkle and for a brief moment the thundering ice and wind stopped, giving Saga a clear view of the mountain peak. There was one narrow path that wound along the peak, from the magical entrance to the ice castle up to the highest tip of the mountain, where a set of strange instruments was bolted to the rock. Empty ice crystals waited beneath. So *this* was how the sorcerers sucked the magic from the Northern Lights, then. It was impossible to see unless you stood on the top of the mountain and she guessed that she was the first person who wasn't a sorcerer to come here in a long time, maybe ever. No wonder nobody knew how they did it. She could also see straight through the window of the turret just below, where shelves of filled ice crystals glimmered.

But the most terrifying sight of all was the figure standing on Bifrost.

It was a frost giant. As huge as a god, with frosted blue skin and three times as tall as the biggest troll she'd ever seen. Saga gulped back a scream – the world of the frost giants was not one that was attached to the rainbow bridge, so if a frost giant was standing on it now, something terrible had gone wrong.

She quickly inscribed another rune without thinking. This time, she carved the two mountains into the snow again, but she added a window and a sun.

A beam of light almost as bright as Bifrost shot out. Dazzled, Saga scrambled back from it on her hands and feet, her magical shield crackling and spitting around her. The sorcerer and frost giant both reared back from the light, and all at once Saga realized her colossal mistake: she'd wanted illumination that came in the form of understanding, not pure light.

With the shield protecting her eyes, she looked directly into the light as the sorcerer turned round, a hand above his eyes. It was Rollo. In his other hand was a horn of ice crystals that he was holding out to the frost giant. A couple fell to the snow as the sky cracked in two with thunder, tossing more wind down until the mountaintop swirled with snow. Saga yelped. Before Rollo could seize an ice crystal to fight against the light and set eyes on Saga, a flock of Arctic terns descended. They swooped low and fast, cutting through the storm to hide Saga with their white wings, their feathers aflutter.

Two pairs of arms reached for Saga.

Canute and Ruvsá dragged her away from the shining rune, running back along the narrow path and jumping down the hole back to the ice castle, Bjørn butting his head into her side to hurry her along.

The magical ring of ice crystals caught them in mid-air, slowing their fall to a controlled float until their boots and paws were all safely back on solid ice inside.

Saga blinked hard to clear the bright spots from her eyes. 'You came!' she said happily.

'We couldn't let you go alone.' Ruvsá hugged her.

'Did you call the birds down?' Saga asked, hugging her back.

'Of course.'

A smile peeped across Canute's face. 'We knew you'd need us, and we were right,' he teased and Saga grinned.

With a flash of clarity, she remembered the seer's words, back in her witch-cave. That the bravest hero did not tread their path alone. That had been before the seer had sent Saga on her way to enter the contest and she suddenly wondered if the seer had known Ruvsá and Canute would be waiting for her, their destinies interwoven like thread. This was followed by a pinch of anger: the seer must have known all along exactly where Afi and Dag were, and had sent Saga to the ice castle not for the contest but to discover the secret hidden down in the mines. She really wished seers would just tell you what was happening without all the mysterious advice.

'Was that a god I saw?' Canute asked, more seriously.

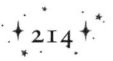

Saga shook her head. 'That was no god – that was a frost giant.' She'd heard enough of Afi's stories to be able to tell the difference.

'So Rollo was talking to a frost giant?' Ruvsá pushed her fur hood back to listen better. Her brown hair slipped free around her face. 'What happened to Vigga's guard?'

Saga shrugged. 'I don't know, but I have more to tell you. Not here, though.' She glanced over her shoulder. 'Let's hurry in case he follows us!'

They fled back through the ice castle, only slowing when they reached the great hall.

There, they were met by another sorcerer.

CHAPTER TWENTY-EIGHT
THE FATE OF THE NORTH

If Saga had thought Vigga was old, then this sorcerer was ancient. He was wizened like tree bark, with drooping ears and a silver beard that trailed on the floor. His stare in their direction was as mottled as a cloud, though his ice crystal, dangling from his forehead band, was the largest gemstone Saga had seen, and it shone with the strength of a hundred stars. Something about that made Saga cautious not to underestimate him. If the seer had taught her anything, it was that power did not fade with age – it only grew more potent.

The three children and Bjørn froze in place, waiting for him to speak. Yet no words came.

'Let's sneak away. He hasn't noticed us yet. Maybe he's blind,' Canute whispered loudly. Ruvsá gave him a pained look as Saga cringed.

The sorcerer gave a throaty chuckle as he peered closer at the children. 'There's still some sight left in this old man yet.'

Canute's cheeks turned pink.

'This post has been abandoned – I can't think why,' the sorcerer muttered to himself, thickening the shield that rippled over the windows as lightning speared through the sky. It was chased by a deafening boom of thunder. 'Whatever was Rollo thinking? I haven't seen a storm such as this since I was a young man.' Unlike the other sorcerers, he did not use an extra ice crystal, nor carve any rune, but wielded the magic with his bare hands, his palms crackling silver-bright. His pickaxe was made of older wood than those of the other sorcerers, his name engraved in gold like Vigga's had been, though this one's runes spelled *Baldr*.

Saga exchanged a significant look with Ruvsá. They knew *exactly* where Rollo had gone, and that he had created the storm himself so that he could sneak up to Bifrost and let a frost giant on to the bridge, but did this mean that Baldr didn't know what was happening in the ice castle?

Baldr whipped back round. 'Have you noticed that there are no trees on these islands?'

Saga cleared her throat, trying to shift her panic. It didn't seem like they were in trouble. 'Yes?'

'Trees cannot survive here. This land is too wild, too uncontrollable . . .' He trailed off as if lost in thought.

'Well, we'll be on our way, then,' Saga said nervously, pulling Ruvsá and Canute towards the narrow ice hallway that held their rooms. Bjørn padded after them.

'Farewell and good fortune with your next task!' Baldr replied jovially, his magic fizzing and spitting in his hands.

Closing the door to her room, Saga turned to Ruvsá and Canute, who were lowering their hoods and shrugging their furs off in front of the crackling purple fire. Their faces were reddened from the wind's vicious bite.

Saga took a deep breath. 'I have something I need to tell you.' She pulled her mittens off.

Ruvsá frowned. 'Your hands are really red – did you take your mittens off up on the peak?'

'Only to draw the runes –' Saga flexed her fingers. They were stiff and she couldn't feel her little finger at all. A fisherman from her village who had lost three fingers to the cold last year popped into her head, and her face flushed hot with panic as she met Ruvsá's worried gaze.

'They'll be fine,' Canute said, surprisingly reassuring. 'Let's go and warm them up in the hot springs.'

*

Saga sat down on a large rock next to a midnight-blue pool that smelled like a forest and now and then blew huge shimmering bubbles. Dangling her bare feet in the steamy water, she finally told her new friends her secret. 'I have a magical destiny,' she cringed; hearing it spoken aloud was every bit as embarrassing as saying it. 'It doesn't mean I think I'm extra special or anything,' she added quickly, 'but a seer visited my family when I was a baby and told them that they had been foretold about me.'

'I thought you were special anyway,' Ruvsá said, nudging her with a smile.

Canute looked as if he really wanted to roll his eyes, but, since they'd become friends, Saga had learned that most of his boasting and annoyingness was just his own shield, protecting the secret of the boy who could turn into a dragon. He settled for asking, 'What did the seer see?'

This was the part Saga had been dreading. She watched Bjørn floating in the water with only his head and all four paws visible, his eyes sleepily blinking back at her. 'They said that I would dream magic and that I held the fate of the North in my hands.'

There was a long silence, filled only with bubbling water and happy bear splashes. Saga shuffled on the rock, waiting.

'Dream magic.' Ruvsá looked thoughtful. 'That must be about your rune dreams, Saga.'

Canute nodded. 'And it explains why you were the one to discover the villagers in the mines and then Rollo speaking to a –' he lowered his voice, looking around the darkly glimmering cave as if someone might pop out of the shadows – 'frost giant.'

'But what does it mean?' Saga asked. 'Do all the sorcerers know about the villagers in the mine and the frost giants, or is this Rollo's secret plan and the others, like Vigga, are trying to stop him?'

'If we know that Vigga is against Rollo then we know that there are two sides to this,' Ruvsá said slowly, 'but we don't know how many sorcerers are on each side and there's no way of figuring that out.'

Saga wiggled her fingers in the hot steam. They were tingling now, much to her relief. 'The sorcerers all go around with those pickaxes when they're not even the ones working down in the mines. I can't believe that none of the sorcerers would notice that many villagers and trolls coming and going down there, or that somehow none of the sorcerers are needed down in the mines, even though the ice crystals keep coming –' She stopped, remembering that Rollo had been handing the frost giant a horn crammed to the brim with ice crystals. 'The ice crystals!'

'What?' Canute asked, alarmed.

'That's the missing link between the two mysteries! They're trying to fill as many ice crystals with magic as possible. That's why they're taking villagers to mine more and more.' Nerves fluttered in Saga's stomach like a seabird's wings. 'So they can give them all to the frost giants.'

Canute made a strange gulping sound. 'What do they need that much magic for?'

'And why are they giving them to the frost giants?' Ruvsá's brown eyes darkened with fear.

'That frost giant was standing on Bifrost,' Saga whispered. 'The sorcerers must be helping the frost giants march on the gods by arming them with magical ice crystals, and if they do –'

'Then the worlds will collapse,' Canute finished.

Bjørn whimpered.

This was an even bigger problem than Saga had imagined – much bigger than saving her afi and Dag. She stood up. 'Then we have to stop them!'

CHAPTER TWENTY-NINE
SAGA, THE STORY SPINNER

Torben laughed so hard he choked on his porridge. Slamming a hand down on the breakfast table, making the plates of bread and salted fish jump, he cleared his throat. Saga waited for him to finish wiping the tears that had sprung from the corners of his eyes. It was morning in the great hall and, after a few fitful hours' sleep, Saga had impatiently waited just long enough for the remaining assortment of raiders, shieldmaidens, Sámi and wanderers to be deep in their plates before approaching Torben with Canute.

While Torben laughed, Saga glanced back at her own seat in time to spot Bjørn sneaking a paw into a bowl of honey. Ruvsá was sitting next to him, pretending to eat porridge while keeping an eye on the sorcerers. Canute was standing awkwardly at Saga's side.

Outside, the storm was tiring at last. It had raged against the sorcerers' magical shield all night, as if Thor was throwing a temper tantrum, making the great walls of ice creak and groan. When Saga had finally got back to bed, she'd lain awake, imagining the whole castle shattering. Although now she wondered if Rollo had stopped funnelling his magic into the storm because he had achieved what he'd wanted to; the storm had distracted everyone enough for him to sneak up to Bifrost by himself and hand over that horn of glimmering ice crystals. When she'd finally fallen asleep, her dreams had been wild and peculiar, of windows that shimmered with memories, and runes that let you soar over the tundra on invisible wings.

'Ah, that's a fine imagination you have there. One for a future bard or story weaver,' Torben managed at last. 'You really had me believing something was wrong for a moment.'

'It *is* wrong,' Saga burst out. Canute coughed pointedly and Saga lowered her voice to a hush. 'And we need your help. If the sorcerers are mining more and more ice crystals to give to the frost giants and letting them cross Bifrost, then the worlds as we know them are in danger! My afi is down in those mines.' Saga's heart gave a painful thump. It was chased by a bolt of pure, bright anger. 'Maybe there's someone you know down there too. I'm raising an army to free them and put a stop to the sorcerers.'

A cloud of concern passed over Torben's face. This was the second time Saga had seen him look worried in as many days – first when her light-bear had sent Knut flying out of the sledge, and now this. It put Saga on edge; this was a raider who had cheered at entering a white-bear den, who had whooped as he'd leaped into a frozen sea.

'Look, I like you, child,' he began, raking his blond hair back with a curse. 'I even admire you. The things you've done? Tyr knows I wouldn't have had the courage at your age. But this is a dangerous accusation.' He glanced up at the sorcerers. 'At the very least, if you're caught talking like this, you'll be banished from the contest with just one challenge left to go. At the worst?' He shook his head solemnly.

Saga felt as if she was back under the crushing weight of the storm last night. 'You don't believe me?'

At Torben's side, Fenrir's beady eyes tracked their conversation, curious and wary at once.

'I don't know what you've seen or what might be happening,' Torben told her, 'but I'm not prepared to risk my skin for a suspicion. You want my advice? Put this behind you, child, and focus on the final challenge. You're going to need to if you want to tame that wild flame of magic you're kindling there.'

'It's fine – we've still got the shieldmaidens,' Ruvsá whispered when Saga and Canute gloomily returned to her side.

'Saga's scared of them,' Canute whispered. Bjørn was now diving into his second bowl of honey, gleeful that nobody had stopped him yet, but Saga had bigger problems to worry about this morning than sticky paws.

'I am not!' Saga marched over to the shieldmaidens.

Solveig turned to survey her coolly. 'Yes?' The other three shieldmaidens in her warband all stopped what they were doing to listen. All four women had long blonde braids, though Saga wasn't sure if that was natural or if they'd bleached their hair with lye to be more fashionable. They'd outlined their eyes with black kohl, turning their stares fiercer.

'Well, there's something happening in the castle that I think you should know about,' Saga began.

'Oh?' Solveig arched an eyebrow.

Saga thought of Afi and Dag down in the mines and soldiered on. 'You know all those troll raids on villages across the North for the past few years? I found out that the missing villagers have all been brought here. They're working down in the mines so that the sorcerers have hundreds more ice crystals to give to the frost giants and –'

'Relax,' Solveig told her. 'You don't need to tell stories to better your chances at winning. The Fates have already granted you powerful magic. I suggest you work on attempting to control that rather than spinning silly little stories.'

Saga's face burned. She thought hard of how to convince them, but before she could speak again Solveig continued, 'Perhaps then you might return to win a future Fifth Winter.' She leaned in closer to Saga, her armour softly clinking, the scent of the forest and tundra and stars clinging to her braids. 'Because this one is *ours*.'

'Have some cake.' Ruvsá slid a plate stacked high with cardamom cake over to Saga, who had returned to their place, buried her head in her arms and silently screamed in frustration.

The cake was so soft and fluffy that it melted in Saga's mouth, but not even this could cheer her. 'Nobody believes me.' She felt as miserable as the endless black skies and freezing cold outside. 'Maybe we need to start thinking of a different plan.'

'There's still Unn and Leif,' Canute suggested.

The three children peered down the table at them. Their heads were bent together, ignoring the food in favour of what looked like a serious conversation.

'Maybe –' Saga began.

Holger chose that moment to stand on the sorcerers' podium. The contestants' attention all flickered to him. He folded his hands over his blue robes, steadily gazing out. His short hair gleamed a brighter silver under the lanternlight, the blue runes on his cheeks shimmering with magic. 'I am pleased to inform you that the storm is waning and we shall be able to reconvene with the third and final challenge tomorrow. Do enjoy your last day in the castle – this final challenge shall not be as easy as the ones you have faced so far.' With that, he sat, resuming his feast with the other sorcerers.

Canute gave him an indignant look. '*Easy?* Easy! He thought those were easy?'

Ruvsá grimaced. 'It's been nice not having to worry about another challenge. I kind of hoped the storm would last another couple of days ... Saga? What's wrong?'

Saga almost couldn't hear her over the roar of panic in her ears. She'd been concentrating so hard on recruiting other warriors to take on the mountain trolls and sorcerers, on the battle brewing between the frost giants and the gods, and her own place in it all with the seer's prophecy thundering through her thoughts – *she will hold the fate of the North in her hands* – that she'd completely forgotten she'd have to compete in another challenge soon.

While the rest of the contestants lingered over the breakfast feast, Saga and her friends sneaked away.

Canute had voted to stay in their rooms, nervous about encountering the sorcerers anywhere else. Saga had made her case for the hot springs, craving the warmth and cosiness of the caves gleaming with lanterns and softly bubbling away. But Ruvsá, who was easily the most persuasive one, had won them both over to her side. Now, they were sitting in the storage cave, with one of Canute's magical fires sizzling in the snow, and a whole cardamom cake shared out between the four of them.

'We don't need another task,' Saga was saying. 'We need to figure out how to persuade the others that I'm telling the truth!'

'And I agree,' Ruvsá repeated, 'but this challenge is going to happen first and you still need to compete in it.'

Canute nodded, spraying cake crumbs everywhere as he agreed. 'She's right, Saga. You can't leave now that your afi is right here, but if you don't compete the sorcerers won't let you stay in the castle!' He jerked his head at the patch of snow in front of Saga. 'Now, have another go. You can do it.'

Saga breathed deeply. She smelled the bite of snow, the fustiness of the cave, the spices in the cake.

'Calm your mind and focus,' Ruvsá said.

Saga let the world melt away: the cave, the occasional rumbles of thunder in the distance, her worries and fears that were all knotted together in one tight tangle. She let go of all of them, until it was only her and the sound of her breath, a steady wave rippling on to a calm shore.

When everything had fallen away, she reached out a single hand and drew a rune in the snow. Two mountains with a window and a sun. The one that had cast its blinding light across the mountaintop last night.

She heard Canute suck in a breath, Bjørn's wary growl, Ruvsá's soft words in her own language. When Saga opened her eyes, there was a window shimmering in the air in front of her. Just like the one she'd seen in her dream. Its edges were blurred, but if you looked straight into it you did not see the cave with its shelves filled with pots, meats hanging to cure, baskets of vegetables and salted fish drying. No, you saw into the past.

'It's my memory,' Saga whispered, watching as the window showed Ruvsá and Canute what had happened last night, the conversation she'd overheard with Vigga and Holger, the mountain troll and villagers in the mine, her afi suddenly staring up at her, horrified as he realized that his granddaughter had entered the mines, then the mountaintop, with Rollo and the frost giant and the ice crystals.

'You know what this means, don't you?' Ruvsá turned to Saga with shining eyes.

Saga nodded. 'This is it. This is how I convince the others that I was telling the truth.'

CHAPTER THIRTY
THE NIGHT OF THREE

That night, three things happened.

First, the storm stopped.

His ears twitching, Bjørn noticed straight away. With a tap of his paw and a gentle huff, he told both Saga and Ruvsá.

'What is it?' Saga glanced up from her nest of furs in their room, where she was experimenting with her runes. Now that she felt more confident in them and herself, she didn't need to practise somewhere else. She'd been drawing the rune for the light-bear, making it smaller and smaller until a tiny bear of light ran and danced over her hand, leaping between her fingers. When she fluttered her fingers and pointed, she discovered that she could guide the light-bear's path, which would be very useful. When she calmed her inner storm to focus on an object, the light-bear was even able to fetch it. She was now sitting next to a small pile of things: her reindeer-antler comb, a chunk of leftover cardamom cake, her mittens, her knapsack and her afi's dagger. She was twisting the dagger this way and that, making the blade twinkle in the light-bear's rays, and wondering if she could sneak down into the mines to visit Afi and Dag and maybe take them some cake, when Bjørn tapped her boot and huffed at her.

'Listen,' Ruvsá said from her own bed, where she had been combing her hair. 'It's the storm – it's stopped.'

Bjørn went trundling over and lay a concerned paw on Ruvsá's arm. 'I'm all right.' Ruvsá half laughed, petting him. 'Maybe we'll finally get a good night's sleep now.' Contented, Bjørn huddled up at the girls' feet and closed his eyes. It wasn't long before sleep stole away Saga and Ruvsá too, curled up together like two crescent moons.

Second, Saga dreamed of runes again.

She was standing on the top of a mountain, drawing a rune. Its shape was the wingspan of an eagle, the edge of a cloud. For the first time, Saga did not feel the cutting fear the runes used to hold for her, not even a tickle of nerves. No, she felt the cry of war before a battle, the spark on a stone that grows a flame. If the raiders and the shieldmaidens did not wish to join her in this fight, then she would bring the fight to them, would show them that there was no other path to tread. More than Afi and Dag's lives were at stake now. The very material of Midgard, their world, could crumble and turn to ash. Dream-Saga's shield fizzed around her, and, closing her eyes, Saga suddenly felt how all the magic was connected. Each rune was like a thread and the worlds a tapestry. She only needed to craft the right threads, the right colours, and she could create whatever she needed. Like the rune she'd cast on the mountain-top that she hadn't needed to dream first.

When dream-Saga opened her eyes, she was flying.

Third, in the thickest part of the night, when time seems to play tricks on your mind and the shadows dance in the corners of the room, there came a knock at the door.

When Saga opened it, Unn stood there.

'I heard what you told Solveig and her warband,' Unn said. Her red hair was unbound, a shawl clasped round her shoulders over her brown leather tunic. 'And I believe you.'

Saga held the door open for her to come in.

Unn folded herself neatly beside the fire, rolling up the sleeves of her tunic to reveal pale, freckled arms, with runes that had been painted on with wood ash. Ruvsá was sitting up in her furs. Bjørn, now that the knock on the door had proved not to be a threat, had fallen back asleep and was snoring loudly.

Unn smiled at him. 'You are greatly fortunate to have such a companion.' She pulled a face. 'Though Leif snores as loudly as a bear, he is not half as adorable. Nor as fierce.' She fixed her spring-green eyes on Saga. 'And I need someone fierce.'

Saga felt more awake at once. 'Tell us.'

'I have been looking for an entrance to the mines since I first arrived at this castle a few days before you.' Unn kneeled forward and cast a quick rune over the fire. It blazed upward at once, its flames heating the room until it was as warm as the hot-spring caves. 'Why did you both venture to the Far North?' she asked. 'It must have been difficult to manage, though I suppose you possess a lot of powerful magic between the three of you. Still, you were lucky to make it all the way up here.'

Saga looked at Ruvsá, who shrugged.

'We had our reasons,' Ruvsá said carefully.

Unn sat back on her heels. 'See, I never set out with the intention to enter this contest. Though I am a student of runes –' she tapped one of her rune-painted arms – 'I am not fortunate to be especially skilled with wielding them magically.' She sighed roughly. 'No, when Leif and I journeyed to the Far North, it was because we were tracking a tribe of mountain trolls.'

Saga stiffened.

Noticing her reaction, Unn nodded. 'That's right. Our village was attacked by mountain trolls, who took most of our people away. Including Leif's wife and my partner, Frida. Leif and I were spared because we were away with a hunting party; both of us are excellent trackers. When we returned to discover our village had been raided, the pair of us set out at once. We tracked the trolls further north, careful to stay half a day's walk behind them lest the wind changed and blew our scent in their direction. Trolls have an exceptional sense of smell,' she added. 'Imagine our surprise when they left the land behind for a great raft, which they sailed to the Far North, landing on this very island, and taking the caught villagers into the sorcerers' ice castle.' She shook her head angrily.

'Do you know which sorcerers know about the villagers in the mines?' Saga asked.

Unn's anger faded to tiredness. Her eye bags were the colour of crushed berries, her hair tangled from where she'd spun it round her fingers as she talked. 'Oh, Saga, they all know.'

Saga slumped with disappointment. Every time she found out something new, it was worse than she'd imagined.

'When you went down to the mines, did you see a woman with short blue braids?' Unn asked.

'I'm sorry. I wasn't down there long enough and I had to leave in a hurry.' Saga fidgeted in her furs.

'Of course.' Unn took a deep breath and composed herself. 'Now, what were you telling Torben and Solveig about the sorcerers and Bifrost?'

Saga shifted into a more comfortable position. 'I can do better than that – I can show you.' She drew the window-rune again, its lines smoother and faster since she'd practised down in the storage cave with her friends. A moment later, the window appeared as if she'd cut it out of the air, shimmering with the light of Saga's memories. Unn's eyes grew larger and larger as she watched Saga's journey down to the mines then up to the mountain peak and what she had discovered there.

When it had played through Saga's memory, the window vanished, leaving the air around it rippling. Unn stared at the space where it had been. 'This –' she gestured at it – 'this is *exactly* what you need to show Solveig and Torben and the rest of the warriors. This is your proof.'

Ruvsá nodded. 'That's our plan. After the next challenge –'

'No,' Unn interrupted. 'If having my Frida taken away has taught me anything, it is that time is precious. And you cannot wait for this. Yes, perhaps Vigga would be on our side, but the rest of the sorcerers are not, and if we wait until after the final challenge we will all be starting to journey home again. No, we need to act now, while we still have warriors here.'

'I agree,' Saga told her. While the idea was scary, it was even scarier to think of something happening to Afi before she'd had a chance to save him. Scarier still to think of the look on his face if he found out she'd known about the frost giants' impending attack on Asgard, the realm of the gods, and done nothing to stop them. After all, she had a magical destiny and now it was calling her. 'Let's make a plan – a proper one.'

'Good,' Unn said, her mouth twitching into a devious smile. 'This seems like the right time to mention that I happen to know exactly what the next challenge will be *and* where it will take place. You're not the only ones who have spent their time snooping around the castle. Though I didn't manage to find the mines, I did discover something useful.'

CHAPTER THIRTY-ONE
THE LAST WINGED HORSES

When the sorcerers' sledge soared over the snow the next morning, Saga stood at the back, watching as the ice castle was lost to darkness. It felt wrong leaving Bjørn behind once more. A silver coin of a moon hung heavy in the sky, and now and then there was a sparkle of green as the Northern Lights played hide-and-seek with the clouds. If all went according to plan, the next time she saw the castle she'd be returning with a small army of warriors at her back, drumming their weapons on their shields as they prepared for battle.

The sledge flew further across the tundra than they'd been before, until its lanterns shone on something looming in the horizon: mountains. Saga watched them inch closer.

'What's wrong?' Ruvsá asked.

'I hope this works,' Saga whispered. 'Because if it doesn't –' She gulped back the words, afraid that if she said them out loud they'd come true.

'It will.' Ruvsá lowered her voice. 'This time, the challenge won't be a surprise. We know what's coming.'

Saga nodded, hoping that Unn was right, and that the task she'd found out about from stealthily tracking the sorcerers around the castle hadn't changed.

'You know –' Ruvsá sidled a look at Saga – 'when my family brings our reindeer herd down from the mountains each winter, we are only a little way along the fjord from your village.'

Saga brightened. 'When we're back home again, when all of this is over, could I come and visit you?' she asked shyly.

'Of course!' Ruvsá beamed. 'Snowflake would love to see you again.' She giggled at the look on Saga's face. 'And I wouldn't mind it either.'

When the sledge began to slow, sinking lower in the air, the foothills of the mountains stretching like bony fingers towards them, Rollo stepped forward. 'These mountains harbour the last colony of winged horses residing in the Far North,' he announced in his silky voice. It was an effort for Saga not to glare at him. She wanted to scream and shout and stamp her foot that this sorcerer was giving magic to frost giants so that they might march across Bifrost and bring war to the gods, threatening that delicate balance between all the worlds.

'Stop it,' Canute whispered to her.

'Stop what?'

He jerked his head at Unn. 'Remember what you told me Unn said: you need to stay focused to wield the magic you practised last night.' Saga and Ruvsá had found out that Leif had had a similar conversation with Canute while Unn had been in their room. The three children had updated each other in whispers over a simple breakfast much earlier than usual that morning.

'It's hard to be calm when I'm so angry all the time. I feel like there's a fire burning in the pit of my stomach,' Saga told him.

'I know.' Canute bumped his shoulder against hers. 'But that is the cost of having such a great gift from the gods,' he teased.

But Saga wasn't in the mood to be teased. She was frightened for her afi, for Dag, for everyone, that the fate of the North rested in her hands. Such a fate was too heavy for her to hold alone, especially when she had never wanted it. It wasn't fair. What if she made a mistake? They were talking about the gods and frost giants and Bifrost and the entire North – this was too big and scary for one girl who had never wanted to run away on an adventure. All Saga had ever wanted was to stay at home and listen to her afi's stories by firelight.

Saga bit her lip as if she could bite her words back, but they came anyway, spilling out of her mouth before she'd properly thought about them. 'If you really think that, then why did you enter this contest to try to get rid of your own powers?'

Canute jolted as if she'd hit him.

'I'm sorry,' Saga said at once. 'I didn't mean it. I –' but Canute shifted away from her, and Rollo chose that moment to continue.

'We have decided to make this challenge a little more . . . interesting.' Rollo's smile was sharkish.

Saga's fear sharpened. It grew into a beast with claws and talons that scratched at her insides and whispered that this plan was too daring, that the raiders and shieldmaidens would never follow her into battle, no matter what proof she showed them against the sorcerers. She closed her eyes and listened to Rollo tell the other contestants the same words Unn had told her and Ruvsá last night:

'This challenge shall be a race. The first contestant to reach the winged horses' lair and ride one of the creatures back to this sledge will be granted that horn of ice crystals you all ventured up here to try to win.'

Saga listened to the contestants' reaction. It was quieter than she'd expected. Maybe that was because the remaining fifteen were more confident. But this challenge could only have one winner, meaning that Unn had been right: Saga couldn't wait any longer.

'Is that all?' Torben asked, sounding puzzled. 'That doesn't sound too difficult.'

Rollo's grey eyes gleamed. 'Then you are underestimating the nature of a winged horse. Believe me when I tell you they bear no resemblance to the gentler-natured horses you find down south.'

Winged horses. The same challenge that had sent Saga's mother out of the contest and into her father's arms, waiting outside the castle for her. Saga wished she'd heard more of her mother's stories now so that she could know what to expect. Before Unn had told her that winged horses were real and she would be expected to ride one, Saga had presumed they simply didn't exist any more.

'The talisman you collected on your first task will enable us to track your progress,' Rollo continued. Before anyone had a chance to ask another question, he then blew a horn, its call echoing around the mountains.

Saga's eyes flew open again. 'Canute, wait,' she pleaded, but Canute shook his golden hair out of his hat, crouched down and leaped up. As he jumped high from the sledge, red-gold scales rippled along his skin as he slipped into his dragon form. The other contestants, setting out from the sledge at a run, glanced up, darkly muttering.

'Let him go,' Ruvsá said. 'I'm sure he won't be cross for long. And you need to hurry if you want to be first there.'

Saga nodded. 'I remember the plan.' She yanked off her mittens and drew a rune in the air, so fast and smooth it was hard to remember when she had been terrified of them. Though she'd only dreamed this rune last night, it was seared into her mind as if she'd studied it all her life. With the wingspan of an eagle and the edge of a cloud, her legs turned feathery light and she began to float.

'Well, that's not fair,' one of the shieldmaidens grumbled as she soared up, up, up into the sky, chasing after Canute.

Flying felt like a dream. Even though magic had stopped being scary for Saga, maybe now it could start being fun. She smiled as she flew up into the mountains, her fingertips brushing against a cloud. Stars twinkled in the gaps between clouds, lighting her way, and she wondered for a moment what she could do if she had some of those ice crystals. Would she be able to fly high enough to touch the moon? She shook the thought from her head, her memories flickering back to her parents' last, terrible blast of magic, and the funeral pyre that had blazed as her afi pushed their boat out to sea one last time. Too much power was never good. And that was why she was going to put a stop to the sorcerers meddling in a rivalry between powerful beings that were older than these mountains.

Canute was still flying ahead of her, which was *not* the plan. Saga gritted her teeth, cross with herself for speaking without thinking. She'd have to hope that she could manage to find the right words this time, when everyone was counting on her.

She slowed, casting a little light-bear. 'Show Canute the right path,' she whispered to it, sending it soaring after Canute until its spark faded in the distance. She couldn't see Ruvsá anywhere, but she didn't worry – Ruvsá's magic was stronger and steadier than hers and Canute's, for all animals in the world would rush to her side in a moment if she needed them. Saga trusted that Ruvsá was busy working on the second part of their plan, and she forged ahead with the first part.

When she glanced down, the other contestants looked like tiny figures below. Saga picked a mountain at random and flew towards it, casting a second, larger light-bear to draw attention to her. As planned, the contestants pursued her, guessing that Saga could see the winged horses from above and would lead them towards victory. But there were no winged horses on this mountain. Saga had something different in mind for them.

She slowly drifted down to the mountaintop, waiting for the contestants to arrive so that she could put the next part of the plan in motion.

CHAPTER THIRTY-TWO
MORE THAN A STORY

Solveig was the first to arrive on the mountaintop, Torben nipping at her heels.

'There aren't any winged horses here,' Solveig said, casting a shrewd eye over the flat expanse of snow Saga was standing on. Her light-bear was perched on her shoulder like a fallen star, but Saga wished Bjørn could have been here too. She was incomplete without him. With a deep crunch, Solveig stood her shield in the snow, before folding her arms over her armour and furs. 'Explain yourself, child.'

Torben turned wary. 'This wouldn't happen to have anything to do with those stories you've been spreading around the castle, would it?'

Saga held her chin high and proud. 'Yes.' Behind Solveig and Torben, she noticed Fenrir step up on to the peak, followed by a couple of shieldmaidens, their identical blonde braids and fur hats making them hard to tell apart.

Torben groaned in frustration. 'I tried to warn you, but you didn't listen. Stories have a way of spinning out of control. It starts with a rumour, a whisper into a friend's ear. Then it grows. Soon, the whisper becomes a shout that your enemies hear, and your secrets are no longer your own.'

'This is more than a story.' Saga drew herself as tall as she could, her magical shield fizzing to life around her. Behind Torben, Saga noticed Leif climb on to the peak, pulling a red-faced, wheezing Unn up after him. Unn nodded fiercely at Saga, coming to stand beside her, and Saga's shield blazed as bright as her determination. Solveig raised a hand to her eyes to ward off its glare. 'I can prove it to you,' Saga said. 'This is the truth.' Before anyone could object, Saga drew her memory rune.

With a ripple of magic, the window appeared and Saga's memories were revealed where the cold, tired raiders and shieldmaidens and trackers could witness them. Saga did not watch again. Instead she kept her stare firmly on the contestants. She noticed Torben's guilty glance back at her and Solveig's stony expression that revealed nothing. The final raiders and last shieldmaiden who quietly joined partway through, falling silent as they caught sight of the shimmering memory window and the events that had spilled across another mountaintop just two nights ago. Of sorcerers and frost giants and mountain trolls and captive villagers.

When Saga's memories had finished, the window vanished, dappling the air like a lake filled with fish.

Solveig was the first to shatter the silence. 'Is this the truth? Or another story?'

'You know magic does not lie,' Torben said quietly. 'That was a memory.'

Solveig snorted. 'Well, we all suspected the sorcerers were corrupt, didn't we?'

'Too much power,' Fenrir growled, shaking his grey mane. 'It's never wise to give a human the power of a god. Goes to their head, it does. Just look at this mess we're in.'

Saga's hopes gleamed brighter. 'Now that you've all finally seen the truth, you must help me stop the sorcerers and rescue the villagers. The balance of the worlds is at stake and if we don't succeed we might lose everything that we love. Every*one*,' Saga added softly, thinking of her afi and Dag, of Unn's partner, Frida, and Leif's wife. So many different stories were tangled together and they needed to fight as one if they wanted a happy ending.

Torben and Solveig exchanged a long look that Saga itched to understand.

'I am mighty sorry that I didn't believe you when you first tried to tell me this,' Torben told Saga gruffly.

'That's all right,' she said quietly.

'It isn't. But I'm going to put things right now,' he said before turning to his band of raiders. 'Upon our honour, we cannot let this stand,' he roared. 'It is our responsibility to protect the villages of the North, and under our watch our people have been taken from under our noses!' He slammed his axe against his shield with a loud boom that reverberated over the mountain.

The raiders roared back. Saga grinned at Unn, who looked as if she might faint with relief.

'You liberate the mines and face off against the mountain trolls, then,' Solveig interrupted, watching him lazily. 'My warband will deal with the sorcerers and frost giants.'

Torben looked at her incredulously. 'How are four of you going to take on an entire castle of sorcerers? Have you ever seen a frost giant? They're as big and mighty as a god, and as tough as a mountain troll. You might wear armour under your furs, but underneath it all you're as soft-shelled as any mortal human.'

Solveig's glare back at him could have sent an avalanche tumbling through the mountains. 'Oh, do tell me what brilliant and courageous plan you've thought up, then,' she spat back.

'Actually,' Unn interrupted, 'Saga has a plan.' She rested a hand on Saga's shoulder, giving it a reassuring squeeze. 'And, since it was down to her that you all know what's been happening in the castle while you've been feasting and bathing in the hot springs, I strongly suggest you listen to her.'

One by one, everyone's eyes fell on Saga.

Just as the enormity of leading a small army into a magical battle against trolls and giants and sorcerers hit her, so did something else. Snow. It was swirling over the mountaintop, churned up by the wind-rush of a huge pair of wings that were flapping in the sky behind Saga. She whirled round. Dragon-Canute was beating his leathery wings as he landed on the mountain, his crimson scales aglow in the moonlight. When Canute screeched, the sky seemed to tremble. Walking on his wing joints and talons, he came to Saga's side and lowered his head, gazing at her with liquid-black eyes.

He'd returned. He must have forgiven her, then. Having a friend at her side gave Saga the surge in courage she needed. She grinned at him before turning back to the warriors and shieldmaidens shifting uneasily in the presence of the dragon.

Putting her hands on her hips, Saga took charge. 'Solveig, I need you and your shieldmaidens to distract the sorcerers. Are you able to take on any frost giants that might appear?'

Solveig inclined her head.

'Good,' Saga said, believing her. The shieldmaidens were *scary*. 'Torben, I need you and your raiders to tackle the mines,' she continued. 'Mount a surprise attack against the trolls and free the villagers.'

'No problem.' Torben puffed his chest out proudly. Fenrir gave a wolfish smile at his side, and the other raiders shouted in agreement as if they were already charging into battle. Solveig rolled her eyes.

'And what are you, our self-appointed leader, going to do?' Solveig asked in a not-completely-nice way.

Saga flushed, but ploughed bravely on. 'First, I'm going to fly to the tip of the ice castle with my friends.' She nodded to Canute; Ruvsá hadn't yet reappeared. 'There, we'll steal a supply of ice crystals. Ruvsá will take them down the castle and divide them between Unn and Leif, who will be ready and waiting. Unn will race down to the mine entrance to give hers to Torben and his raiders, and Leif will rush to get his to Solveig and her warband. That should give you all enough of a magical boost to overpower the trolls and giants. Then Canute and I are going to destroy the supply of ice crystals,' she announced. 'Smash every last one of them until we've robbed the sorcerers of the magic they've promised the frost giants.'

Canute gave a great flap of his wings, screeching into the sky.

Torben was stroking his braided beard. 'I reckon that'll do it.' He grinned slowly. 'You'll make a raider yet, child.'

'With those brains?' Solveig scoffed. 'She's much more likely to be a shieldmaiden.'

Saga's blush deepened with pleasure. In the distance, she heard a musical fluttering that sounded like the wind sighing through the trees back home.

'There's just one snag,' Solveig continued. 'How are you planning to get us to the ice castle without dealing with this challenge or the sorcerers on the sledge, who could send a warning ahead to the castle?'

Saga smiled at her. She turned to look over the mountains, glistening with ice like melted moonlight dripping down their sides. Under the tapestry of clouds and stars, woven together with thready ribbons of the Northern Lights, came what looked like birds.

'With those,' she said.

Fenrir squinted, his bushy grey eyebrows bunching together. 'Are those eagles?'

'No.' Something rose within Saga, fierce and unstoppable as she watched what flew towards them grow larger and larger. 'They're winged horses.'

PART FOUR
THE BATTLE OF RUNES AND ICE

She will hold the fate of the North in her hands.

CHAPTER THIRTY-THREE
TIME TO WIELD WAR

The winged horses looked as if they'd flown straight out of a story.

'Ohhh,' Solveig said in a feather-soft voice.

Their coats were as silver as moonlight, their manes as golden as star glitter and their wings the colour of fresh snowfall. There were more than Saga had imagined, filling the sky with their vast wingspans and sparkling hooves, tossing their glittering manes and neighing. Ruvsá laughed and waved, riding the horse in front. Saga beamed and waved back. The herd circled the mountaintop and landed on the snowy plateau, huffing and snorting. A few raiders stepped back; the winged horses were taller than Bjørn standing on his hindlegs, and more than one had snarled at the nearest raiders, revealing sharpened teeth that shone like lines of tiny swords.

Ruvsá patted the mane of the horse she rode, singing under her breath until it calmed, its violet eyes gentling. It bowed its head, bending its forelegs, and lowered Ruvsá to the ground. When she sang louder, the entire herd copied, letting Saga, Unn and Leif, the raiders and the shieldmaidens mount them.

'Now, we ride!' Saga shouted, thrusting one arm in the air. She reached inside her furs, pulling her talisman out and holding it up before tossing it into the snow. For a moment, it rained talismans as everyone hurried to discard theirs as well. Saga hoped that would fool the sorcerers into believing they were still atop the mountain long enough to give them a head start. 'We need to fly a different route back to the castle,' she said to Ruvsá, who nodded in agreement, 'so that the sorcerers don't see us overhead.'

Ruvsá whispered into her horse's twitching ear, and the creature spread its wings wide and cantered off the mountaintop. A moment later, it reappeared, soaring high. Saga's horse copied, her stomach swooping as it leaped into the air, then again as the current caught its wings and they flew on.

With a battle cry, the rest of their army followed. Canute spread his own wings, joining them in the sky.

*

The moon and stars lit their way through the dark skies. When Saga glanced at Ruvsá's horse, it looked back at her, its teardrop-shaped violet eyes filled with the reflection of a hundred stars. She was sad that this was the last colony of winged horses; they were beautiful and majestic, and deeply intelligent, though she hoped she'd never be at the biting end of those sharpened teeth. Saga and Ruvsá smiled at each other, riding side by side back to the ice castle, the wings of their horses nearly touching. 'They're a pair,' Ruvsá told her, stroking her horse's mane. 'Sisters.'

'Like us,' Saga said shyly, making Ruvsá beam brighter than the moon.

Too soon, the ice castle rose into view. Its jagged mountaintop, glistening ice halls and turrets looked like a threat.

Ruvsá guided the flying herd round the back of the castle, where they landed in a flutter of wings and stamping hooves.

'I will show Torben where the trolls first took the villagers inside the mines,' Unn told Saga, 'then I will return to the great hall to wait for you.' She directed the last part to Ruvsá, who laid a reassuring hand on her horse, calming it.

Torben quietly raised his shield and whisper-shouted, 'Tyr!' as he led his band of raiders after Unn.

That was when Saga realized that the warband of shieldmaidens was missing. 'Where did they go?' She whirled around.

'Up there.' Leif pointed at the mountain they stood beside, where Solveig and her three shieldmaidens were using ice picks and daggers to swiftly climb up the ice and breach the castle from the outside. Leif then hurried off to sneak into the castle, where he would be waiting beside Unn.

Satisfied that no sorcerer had yet raised the alarm, Saga climbed back on her winged horse. She gulped in a lungful of freezing air and held on to her horse as it leaped into the air, veering almost vertically up the side of the mountain. Following Ruvsá's horse, the pair soared up past the walls of the ice castle, their wings trailing music that sounded like a dance of silk and snow. Behind them, Saga heard the leathery flap of Canute's dragon wings as he followed the horses at a careful distance.

The tip of the ice castle came into view – the tallest turret where the ice crystals were stashed and guarded – and the mountain peak that rose behind it. Saga's heart thudded like a battleaxe.

It was time to wield war.

CHAPTER THIRTY-FOUR
THE TALLEST TURRET

The winged horses landed on the frozen, slanted roof of the tallest turret, their hooves grappling for purchase on the ice. Saga's shield immediately rippled over her, sending her horse into a neighing panic. It thrashed its golden mane and stamped its hooves as it snapped its sharp teeth together. Saga clung on desperately, but its silky down slipped through her mittens and she fell off its back, careening down the roof.

'Saga!' Ruvsá called after her in alarm.

Before she could think to cast a rune or even scream, Saga's shield clamped down on the ice, sending all the air whooshing out of her lungs as she stopped abruptly just before she fell off the turret. Then Canute swooped down on her, gently hooking his talons through her furs and setting her down beside Ruvsá, who had now dismounted her own horse.

'I'll send them back now,' Ruvsá said, a little sadly, after checking that Saga was unharmed. She whispered into the horses' ears, running her hands through the long, silky manes that reached their hooves. Both horses sprang from the roof at the same time, their wings billowing out like sails as they flew away. The three children watched them, gleaming under the starlight. A heartbeat later, the whole sky filled with winged horses as the rest of the herd joined them, soaring back home together.

'Now we need to sneak into the turret and distract whoever's been left guarding it,' Saga said.

Ruvsá squeaked in alarm. 'I think we're too late for that – look!'

Saga looked down. Vigga was hanging out of the window in the turret and staring directly up at them.

'Uh-oh.' Saga gulped.

'I'd thought that all the contestants were away in the mountains, competing in the final challenge today,' Vigga said when Saga and Ruvsá climbed down the turret roof and swung themselves in through the window. Since Canute hadn't been spotted, he'd slipped quickly out of view.

'Surely you cannot have returned already,' Vigga continued, 'so why did you not leave with the sledge this morning? And whatever could you be doing on this roof?'

'Errr ...' Saga cast around for an excuse. She was distracted by the room in which they stood, the one she had glimpsed that night on the mountain peak, but inside which she'd never been until now. The turret was round and small, though surprisingly high. Its ice wall was thick, with hundreds of cubbyholes where gleaming ice crystals nestled, bursting with magic and ready to be used. Their green-blue glow rippled around the ice as if the Northern Lights were shining brightly inside the turret. A rickety wooden ladder spiralled round and up so that you could reach them all. It was dripping with icicles. There was a hatch on the roof, with a folded ladder to access the mountain peak when it was time to bring the magically charged crystals inside to safety. Saga hadn't noticed this outside, where it was crusted with snow.

'You seem mighty interested in the ice crystals.' Vigga's eyes glinted when Saga tore her gaze away from the store. Vigga stepped closer to her. Ruvsá and Saga bunched together in defence. 'That's why you're here, isn't it? To steal some and use them to win the contest?'

Saga shook her head. 'Not at all –'

Vigga raised an ice crystal from her pocket, holding it threateningly. Saga's shield crackled in response, casting its protective barrier over Saga and then stretching further until it enveloped Ruvsá as well.

Vigga staggered back as the shield glared and spat magic at her.

'That's new,' Ruvsá muttered, touching the shield glimmering around her like a soap bubble.

The door to the turret suddenly flew open, thudding into the ice wall. Standing there was Rollo. Out of breath, as if he'd dashed immediately up to the tip of the castle, he wore a thunderous expression on his face.

'You,' he snarled, looking angrier than Saga had ever seen him before. 'You have a lot to answer for.'

Ruvsá clung on to Saga's arm as Saga's shield burned brighter, preparing to ward off an attack. Saga wondered if Canute was listening in outside.

But Rollo wasn't looking at Saga and Ruvsá. He was looking at Vigga.

'You've come just in time,' Vigga said calmly. 'I caught these children sneaking about on the roof, doubtlessly about to steal some ice crystals for their own use.'

Rollo's eyes flicked to Saga and Ruvsá. He didn't look surprised to see them there. 'That was a nice trick you pulled with the talismans. It took us a while to realize you weren't all still up at the mountaintop. But when nobody returned to complete the task . . .' He shrugged. 'You failed to account for the fact that our sledge is much faster than a winged horse.'

Saga curled her hands into fists. 'I know what you and the rest of the sorcerers are doing,' she snapped at Rollo. 'I overheard Vigga telling Holger all about it and then I saw you on the mountain peak, handing a horn of ice crystals over to that frost giant. Well, good luck getting these to your giant friends now.' With that, Saga whirled round and swept an arm into the nearest cubbyhole teetering with ice crystals. She flung them on to the floor, stamping her boot on top of them until they fractured. But Rollo was not the sorcerer who reacted as she'd expected.

'No!' Vigga snarled, reaching out to grab Saga. 'Stop that at once!'

Vigga's hand jerked to a stop in the air. Her arms snapped to her sides, her legs clamping together as she stood as straight and stiff as a plank of wood, wobbling in place.

Saga stared at Vigga, frozen in front of her, then at Rollo, who had just finished drawing a rune.

'You bound her.' Ruvsá realized first.

Rollo nodded grimly. 'But she is more powerful than me, so we don't have much time. That conversation you overheard with Vigga and Holger, tell me what was said.'

Frowning, Saga quickly told him what she'd heard.

'That explains a lot,' Rollo sighed, raking a hand through his silver hair. 'Vigga is a master manipulator. She's been slowly persuading all the sorcerers to come over to her side, turning them against me, against reason itself.'

'What are you talking about?' Saga narrowed her eyes at him.

'Vigga is not who she seems.'

They all looked at Vigga, who was still bound as if she'd been tied up with invisible ropes, though she could hear everything that was being said, her eyes rolling from side to side as she watched them.

Rollo suddenly turned to Saga. 'That frost giant that you saw me handing a horn of ice crystals to – I was not passing them over but taking them away from it.'

'Why should we believe you?' Ruvsá folded her arms.

Rollo's smile was dangerous, daring. 'Why don't you do what you came up here to do?' he challenged them.

Though Saga didn't trust him and definitely did not want to turn her back to him, she knew that, by now, everyone else would be waiting for her plan to unfold, worrying that something had gone wrong. All it would take was one person to leave their post to check what was happening and the whole plan would crumble to pieces.

'Fine,' she decided quickly, turning to the supply of ice crystals and scooping giant handfuls out. Ruvsá held her pockets and hood open for Saga to fill, the gemstones tinkling together as she crammed as many in as possible.

'Are you sure you're going to be all right?' Ruvsá whispered when they couldn't fit any more in. Her forehead was knotted together with worry. 'I don't want to leave you alone up here.'

'I'll be fine,' Saga told her. 'Go.'

With one last anxious glance back, Ruvsá sidled past Vigga and Rollo, then ran out of the door.

Saga began smashing as many of the ice crystals as she could reach. Soon she would have no choice but to climb the ladder that spiralled up and up, nailed to the ice with iron brackets, but it was bad enough turning her back to Rollo with her feet on the floor.

When each ice crystal smashed, it released a bright spark of light that fluttered away with a little hum before vanishing. Saga kept sneaking glances at Rollo, but he kept his distance, watching her with his arms folded over his chest. Frowning, she turned back to destroying the ice crystals, puzzling over his behaviour. Soon, the turret was filled with fluttering green-blue sparks, the little hums chiming together into a song that filled Saga with hope. Maybe they were wending their way home to their source so that the next time the Northern Lights appeared they would be brighter and more powerful than ever, filling the entire sky with their shimmer.

'You're taking too long,' Rollo said a few moments later, coming to stand beside Saga, helping her scoop armfuls of ice crystals out of their cubbies and on to the floor, then stamping on them until they shattered. If she hadn't completely believed in his innocence before, she did now. Her shield sank back beneath her skin, resting just under the surface.

'Can't we use magic to destroy them?' Saga drew a mitten across her forehead, sweating inside her furs.

'I'm afraid not,' Rollo replied. 'Using magic around them interferes with the magic they hold inside the crystals. They work as an amplifier, so it often has disastrous effects, especially around this many.' He jerked his head back at Vigga. 'That's why I was able to bind her. I could only have done that up here.'

'Why?' Saga asked warily. 'Is it because she's older than you?'

'No,' Rollo said, giving her a funny look. 'It's because she isn't human.'

'Stop!' Vigga suddenly roared, bursting out of her magical bonds.

Rollo snapped to attention, quickly casting another rune as Saga's shield fizzed back to life, fiercer than ever. But Vigga unhinged her jaw and roared again, loud and deep enough to shake the icicles off the ladder.

Saga gaped at her.

'Get back!' Rollo snapped at Saga.

But Saga couldn't move. She was too shocked at the sight of Vigga's face shifting, as if something was moving beneath her skin.

'What *is* she?' Saga shouted. There was a great ripping sound as Vigga's human body tore in half and the monster within rose as if it had been crouching inside its human costume.

'She is the frost giant that you saw,' Rollo said grimly.

CHAPTER THIRTY-FIVE
THE FROST GIANT

Vigga the frost giant roared again. It shook the turret so hard that Saga was scared it would snap off from the ice castle.

'Please tell me that you have a plan worked out and this was not just some valiantly foolish effort that you two girls undertook alone,' Rollo shouted across to Saga, shielding his face from the frost giant as she tossed off the last bits of her sorcerer skin. The giant beneath had pale blue, leathery skin and white eyes, with wickedly curved talons and stubby horns.

'Of course, I have a plan!' Saga shouted back.

'Good. Off you go, then.' Rollo gestured at the open door. 'And I'll finish what you started in here.' He gestured at the ice crystals, though he kept his eyes on the frost giant. 'I've been waiting a long time for this.' His sharkish smile reappeared, making Saga glad that it was directed at the frost giant and not at her for once.

Vigga the frost giant suddenly turned round, fixing her attention on Saga and Rollo. A predator before the pounce. 'How dare you destroy the magic I was promised?' she bellowed.

'Go!' Rollo shouted, and Saga fled.

As she ran through the doorway, she felt the collision between Rollo and Vigga the frost giant thunder around the turret. A deep crack appeared, running through the ice at her feet. Saga leaped over it without thinking, landing awkwardly on her knees and then skidding further along the icy passageway, gathering speed until she collided with something big and fluffy.

'Bjørn!' Saga cried out, throwing herself into his paws.

He snuffled into her hair, holding her tight against his fur.

'Oh, Ruvsá sent you my way, didn't she? I am so happy to see you again.'

An ominous creak rippled through the passageway and Saga clung tighter to Bjørn, who whined anxiously.

'We need to go,' Saga said, climbing back to her feet and breaking into a run, Bjørn at her side. 'It's not enough to destroy the ice crystals,' she panted as she raced through the castle towards the ring of ice crystals that would send them soaring up to the peak. 'We need to get rid of their equipment so they can't make any more. That will slow them down enough for us all to get back home and spread the word of what we've witnessed up here.'

Then maybe the Jarls would band together and send an army up to make sure that this could never happen again. But, most importantly, Saga would be back in her favourite place, with her favourite people. She wondered how the others were getting on, if Torben and his raiders had managed to free the villagers yet or if they were still battling the trolls, if Afi and Dag had left the mines. There was another creak. This one sounded like a huge crust of sea ice breaking apart. It was chased by a roar.

Saga ran faster.

She leaped up into the ring of light, Bjørn right behind her, and burst out on to the mountain peak in time to see Canute standing on top of the turret. His scales were glistening darkly, more like black silk than crimson in the never-ending night. As she watched, he whipped his head back and roared again, summoning an answering roar from the frost giant inside. With the combined weight of the dragon and giant, several deep fractures had appeared where the turret was connected to the castle.

'It's going to fall,' Saga realized. She waved her arms over her head, trying to catch Canute's attention. 'Rollo is still in there!' she screamed up to him. When he snapped his head down, she thought he'd heard her. Instead, he breathed fire on to the turret.

The narrow ice bridge attaching the turret to the castle melted. And the turret slid away from the castle, falling past the outer ice walls and further down the mountain until there was a mighty crash as it collided with the ground as if a god had reached out and thrown it. A cloud of snow and ice flew out from the impact. It was too far away for Saga to see if anyone had crawled out of the wreckage, but, as she watched, an eruption of light and song danced out of the turret, the magic rippling from the smashed ice crystals in one glittering wave.

Saga tore herself away and forged through the snow along the narrow, wind-torn passage that led up to the jagged peak at the tallest point of the mountaintop. Here Bifrost burned a rainbow across the sky to the world of the gods, and the ancient set of instruments were bolted to the mountain rock.

Though Saga squinted at Bifrost, its blazing light thundering with magic, she couldn't see anyone standing on or near it. Its sheer power sent her stomach crawling with nerves, as if her old fear of magic had cracked an eye open after slumbering for days and days. She gritted her teeth and turned her back to it, concentrating on the set of instruments.

They looked as if they could have come from the metal crafting workshop in her village. They were a collection of bottles and pipes and other instruments for which she had no name, and they were made of a strange material she'd never seen before, a blend of metal and glass that shimmered like a pearl yet was as fine as a moth wing. Saga reached out a hand to touch them, confused by how they could possibly be strong enough to stand on top of the mountain without shattering. They were silver-streaked where they had been scorched by raw magic.

'You are drawn to them, are you not?' an old voice creaked behind her.

Saga whirled round.

She was met with Baldr's unseeing stare. Bjørn shuffled uneasily at Saga's side as she tried to work out how the ancient sorcerer had seen her. He was dressed in his robes, missing the thick, fur-lined blue cloak that the other sorcerers wore when venturing outside, but he didn't seem cold even though his silver beard was frozen all the way down to his feet.

'It's perfectly natural,' Baldr chuckled. 'Do you know how I lost my sight?'

'No,' Saga said, fretting that he was about to begin a long, winding tale that would have been boring even by firelight, but unbearable up on the blisteringly cold mountaintop, where she was itching to destroy the magical equipment so that she could race back down and find her afi. She didn't even know if she *could* break this structure, but up here, where the only ice crystals were the horns of empty gemstones, she could use her own magic as a weapon without accidentally destroying anything else.

'I was a mortal who stared at the sun,' Baldr said. He gestured at Bifrost. 'I had just been welcomed at the ice castle – many, many years ago – when I was shown the wonder of the rainbow bridge for the first time. The other sorcerers in training and I were then ushered down to the great hall for our first feast, where their minds turned to stew and roast meat and fresh fruit, and all the foods we had not eaten in our villages since summer. Yet I could not forget what I had seen. I returned alone, later that night, and I did what no mortal ought ever to do.'

'What did you do?' Saga was drawn into his story even as she itched to move.

The large ice crystal at Baldr's forehead gleamed brighter. 'I stepped on to Bifrost.'

Saga was too stunned to speak.

Baldr chuckled again. 'I managed to walk several steps along it before it spat me out. I thought I had fallen face-first into the snow since everything was white. It wasn't until later that I realized what price I had paid for being tempted by that burning light, that incandescent power.' His voice dipped. 'Though I don't need to tell you how that much magic tempted me.'

A shiver darted down Saga's spine. Sensing it, Bjørn growled under his breath.

'What do you mean?' Saga asked.

'Do not mistake my blindness for lack of sight,' Baldr told her. 'Since my gaze turned inward that day, I have seen all. I am able to peer between the branches of the great Yggdrasill tree that holds all the worlds together, seeing into other realms and minds and times.' His feet crunched into the snow as he trod closer to Saga. Her shield hummed to life, Bjørn raising his hackles. 'Yes, I saw your parents' great sacrifice. And further back too, to when you were a tiny mewling thing, scarcely bigger than a kitten, and a seer journeyed across the fjords because she had seen your prophecy written in the stars. *She will hold the fate of the North in her hands.'*

Saga couldn't move or think to speak.

Baldr gestured at the structure behind her. 'Your destiny awaits you. But I do wonder which one you will choose.'

CHAPTER THIRTY-SIX
SAGA'S DESTINY

At last, Saga found her voice. 'What do you mean?'

Baldr's smile was not reassuring. 'If the fate of the North rests in your hands, will you continue on your destructive path, ridding the castle of as many ice crystals as you can, or will you choose another way?'

'It was you,' Saga suddenly realized. 'You were the sorcerer who Vigga – who the frost giant pretending to be Vigga – was talking about. The one who promised her the horns of ice crystals to march on the gods. It was never Rollo – it was always *you*.'

Baldr feigned clapping. 'I was wondering how long it would take you to work that out.'

'I will never join you!' Saga said, appalled that he'd even considered that an option.

Baldr's mottled gaze settled on Saga as if he could see straight through her. 'Ah, I wouldn't be so quick to dismiss that which you do not understand. Magic is power, child. You can't comprehend the things you could achieve with this much power at your disposal.' He gestured at the instruments behind Saga. 'By arming Vigga, a leader of a warband of frost giants, and sending her over Bifrost, the frost giants will be in my debt.' His smile cut wider, his wrinkles sinking deeper. 'And by warning the gods of their impending attack, the gods will then look favourably upon me.'

'You're double-crossing the frost giants?' Saga stared at him, horrified at the thought. 'Aren't you scared they'll find out?'

Baldr didn't seem worried. 'Even if they did, I've already harvested more than enough ice crystals to protect myself.'

Saga gestured at the mountain that sprawled out beneath them. 'Those ice crystals are all smashed at the bottom,' she told him smugly. 'And since the villagers are being freed this very moment from the mines, you'll never be able to make that many again.' She glanced back at the instruments. She needed to hurry up. Smoke was clouding up from below and she guessed that Canute was at the foot of the mountain, still in his dragon form, but she needed to finish with her part of the plan so that she could go and help the others. She hadn't seen the shieldmaidens since they'd scaled the mountain, but now and then a yell or blast of magic shot out of the castle windows below. Battle sounds. She hoped Ruvsá was all right.

'I will with you on my side,' Baldr said. 'I sensed your raw power the moment you first set foot in the ice castle. Together, we could achieve the unthinkable.'

Saga scoffed. 'I'd rather jump off the mountain than give you another ice crystal!'

'Even if it gave me enough power to bend the rules of time itself?' Baldr's voice turned tempting. 'Or bring the dead back to life?'

Saga stilled.

'That's right,' Baldr crooned. 'If you joined me, together our power would be unstoppable, enough to prise open the gates to Valhalla and bring your parents back into our realm. They don't have to stay dead forever.'

Saga's eyes prickled. She hadn't thought that Baldr could ever tempt her with magic, but she hadn't expected this. The idea of seeing her parents again was almost too much to bear.

'You could return home together, be a proper family again,' Baldr said softly. 'You must have missed them terribly.'

Saga missed them so badly it was a constant ache. She suddenly wondered what it would be like to return to her longhouse and see her parents waiting and smiling there, holding out their arms for her to run into again.

'And then there is your grandfather, your bear, your friends,' Baldr continued. 'What would it feel like to know that they could always be safe, that by seizing this magic, this power for yourself, you would be protecting them.'

Saga's ache sharpened. 'It would be wrong,' she whispered.

'Would it?' Baldr stepped closer again. 'Or would it be exactly what they – and you – deserve? To never have to worry again, to spend your days together with your family, your home always safe and healthy and happy.'

Bjørn whined, nudging Saga and bringing her back to her senses with a jolt. She shook her head as if she could shake the temptation out of it. 'It wouldn't be real,' she said, finding her inner strength and drawing on it. 'And it wouldn't be what my parents would have wanted. Or Afi. That power isn't mine to take and it wouldn't be right. It would betray everything my parents have ever stood for and I won't let them come back just to see that their sacrifice was for nothing.' Her voice cracked. 'Even if it means that I never get to see them again.' She paused, blinking hard to clear her eyes. A rising tide of anger caught her unawares. 'How dare you try to use my parents against me?' she growled at the old sorcerer. 'That power isn't for you either.' She turned, already forming the shape of a rune that she held in her head. One that she had not needed to be asleep to dream up.

Too late, she remembered that you should never turn your back on an enemy.

'That power is what I deserve!' Baldr shouted, grabbing Saga's shoulder with a twisted, knotted hand. Bjørn growled, snapping his jaws together, and Saga's shield burst into life, but Baldr's nails were like long claws, painted with runes, and they pierced her shield. She cried out, struggling against him. 'And I will not let any sorcerer, let alone a child, take it from me!' Baldr's nails sank into Saga's furs as she scrabbled at his hand. Bjørn roared and leaped at the old sorcerer, but Baldr shoved Saga, as hard as he could, off the mountaintop.

The ice peak swirled as Saga fell. Her shield slowed her and with a scream of rage, she clawed at the mountain, digging her fingers into the rock until she found a groove. She came to a sudden stop that yanked her arms from her shoulders, leaving her dangling off the edge of the peak. She needed to cast her flight rune, but to do so would mean letting go with one hand and she wasn't sure how quickly her shield could catch her. She didn't want to put it to the test. Nor did she want to leave Bjørn up there alone with Baldr, who she didn't trust. Right now, he could be undoing everything for which she'd fought.

Bjørn's nose appeared above her.

Saga nearly cried with relief. 'I'm down here!' she called.

Bjørn whined and his nose disappeared. A moment later, his paw batted at Saga's hair, then her hood. With his claws hooked through the fur of her hood, Bjørn pulled Saga back up on to the mountain. She hugged him fiercely as he huffed affectionately into her ear.

Baldr looked annoyed.

'You see that?' Saga said triumphantly. 'I don't need magic to save me because I am never alone. Proper families come in all kinds of shapes and sizes, and I love mine, but you're always going to be alone because you only care about power.'

Before he could reply, she cast the rune she'd been holding in her head. At its root was Kenaz, the rune for fire and warmth, that could also sometimes mean craftmanship and physical transformation, the rune that Canute favoured. Then there were branches that were shaped like lightning, and a ripple of the Northern Lights for a cloak of leaves. It was the shape of power, of magic itself, and it blasted across the mountaintop in flames of the purest silver.

Though it was the most powerful magic she'd ever wielded, Saga was not afraid, for at its heart was love.

Her love for her family and friends and everybody she wanted to protect – she was fighting for them now. Saga channelled every last bit of her energy into it, feeding it until the flames turned incandescent. Its fire devoured the light-stealing instruments, their peculiar material warping as the whole structure began to melt, dripping down the peak, scorching the ice and snow with its heat until Saga was standing on rock.

'What have you done?' Baldr fell to his knees, his hands in the air as if he could quench the flames. He seized the ice crystal at his forehead, snapping it off its band and calling on its power as he cast runes for water, for wind, for snowfall. But nothing could quench Saga's fire.

'I have chosen my destiny,' she told him, feeding every last drop of her anger into the magical fire pouring out of her, 'and you are *not* in it.' She fired one last burst of sheer power until the instruments Baldr had been counting on to fuel his magic were nothing but a silver puddle.

Baldr suddenly reared up and began hobbling over the mountaintop as fast as he could, breaking into an uneven run towards Bifrost.

'He's going to try to cross it again,' Saga said out loud. 'What if he manages this time?' Bjørn roared angrily at her side. 'Should we stop him?' Saga asked, but she was starting to feel strange and wasn't sure she could. Using that much magic had drained her. Slumping against Bjørn, she watched as Baldr reached the rainbow bridge, which was too bright to look at. Shielding her eyes with a hand, Saga squinted, just able to make out the bent figure of the old sorcerer walking into the light. He took one step, two, before he stopped. When Saga risked one more peek, she saw another person appear on the bridge – no, not a person. This being was too great in size to be another sorcerer.

'Is that another frost giant?' she whispered, fear gnawing at her.

Then she heard their voice. 'You have threatened our hard-won peace, and the very fabric of the worlds themselves with your own greed, mortal. For that, you shall be punished,' they boomed, making even the burning bridge tremble.

It wasn't a frost giant, it was a *god*. Saga's legs turned to porridge.

And, with that, the god vanished, taking Baldr with them, wherever that might be.

CHAPTER THIRTY-SEVEN
TOGETHER AGAIN

After all the magic she'd used, then hearing the voice of a god so close to where she had been standing, Saga was bone-tired. She leaned against Bjørn, and they slowly made their way back into the ice castle and down through its twisted icy passageways. Together.

In the great hall, they discovered the sorcerers all huddling together, casting terrified looks at the four shieldmaidens that stood over them with their armour glinting in the lanternlight, their swords held high.

'What happened?' Saga asked Solveig.

Solveig shrugged casually. 'Once you make an example of one or two of them, the rest fall in line pretty quickly.'

She tossed an ice crystal into the air and caught it with one hand. 'These helped.'

'Were there any more frost giants?'

'No. Just the one that was trying to claw its way out of the turret as it fell, but your dragon friend took care of that.' Solveig almost looked disappointed.

Saga's smile was tight. She was exhausted and relieved, but her worries were still churning like a rough sea. 'Where's Ruvsá?'

'I haven't seen her,' Solveig said.

'I'm certain she's down in the mines,' another shieldmaiden added. 'As much as he's fond of boasting, Torben and his raiders were incapable of subduing the mountain trolls by themselves.' She shared a smirk with Solveig.

Everything but Ruvsá flew out of Saga's head. 'I have to find her.' She climbed on Bjørn's back, rushing further down the castle, following the frozen maze of passageways and silent halls dripping with icicles, until they'd reached the colder, gloomy lower part, where the castle met the mountain.

There, the door to the mines was hanging off the wall.

Bjørn hesitated. A colossal roar shook the mountain itself and Saga dredged up her last tiny reserve of energy and urged her bear on. Bjørn half slid, half galloped down the slick stairwell and they burst out into the mines, Saga already attempting to conjure her light-bear rune. A tiny pinprick of light emerged with a snout and two ears before fizzling out. Her well had run dry. Instead, Saga reached for her grandfather's dagger, always hidden within her furs, and clenched it while Bjørn cautiously prowled on.

The huge cavern was empty.

As Saga and Bjørn picked their way through it, signs of a mighty battle were everywhere. Smashed ice crystals, overturned sledges, pickaxes embedded in the rock where they had been thrown. A couple of knocked-out mountain trolls were lying there too. When another roar sounded, Saga snapped her head round.

'There!' she told Bjørn, spotting a gaping hole in the wall, ringed with flames.

Carefully placing his paws between the smouldering ruins, Bjørn walked through it with Saga on his back.

They emerged outside.

There, in the snow, the battle was raging to an end.

A great silver fire was still burning, its light dancing over Canute's dragon scales like molten moonlight as he faced off against two of the biggest mountain trolls Saga had ever seen. With seven heads and five arms between them, they bellowed angrily at Canute, tossing huge boulders at him. Canute was incinerating each one with his own fire-breath. At his side fought a lone sorcerer: Rollo. He was limping, but he had survived the fall.

Another troll was using an entire tree as a club, roots and all, batting at a couple of white bears that were pouncing at it. Only one person could have brought bears into the battle.

'Ruvsá,' Saga murmured, searching through the fiery, snowy chaos for her friend. 'She's over there!'

Bjørn huffed, padding quickly to where Ruvsá was hiding behind the fallen turret, guiding the bears to attack.

Saga slid off Bjørn and hurried over.

'Saga!' Ruvsá beamed and threw her arms round her. Saga hugged her fiercely, laughing as Bjørn pushed his nose between them, wanting to be included.

'Look, we did it,' Ruvsá said. 'Your plan worked!' She pointed at a pack of raiders, led by Torben, who were armed with the last of the ice crystals as they chased off another few trolls. The trolls' thundering footsteps felt like an earthquake as they fled, the raiders cheering at their victory. Some of the raiders looked more familiar than she'd expected, and Saga squinted at them. 'Is that . . . my Jarl?'

Ruvsá laughed. 'After we freed the villagers from the mines, quite a few of them wanted to join in the fight.'

Saga looked at them again, realizing that Torben was not only leading raiders but villagers as well. Some of them, like the Jarl, were even from her village. Her gaze turned searching. 'Where's –'

'*Saga*,' a voice said behind her.

It was the voice of bedtime stories, the one that framed her day from dawn to dusk, who made her feel safe, who sent her worries scuttling away, who had taught her how to fight with sword and shield, who made the very best porridge. It was the voice of home. Hearing it again made Saga's heart swell so much that she thought it would burst through her chest.

'Afi,' she gasped, turning and falling into his waiting arms. When they closed round her, she was home again. 'I missed you so much.'

'You have found me.' His arms tightened, his beard tickling her forehead just as she remembered. 'And now we are together again nothing will keep us apart. Saga, my favourite story of all, now you have some stories of your own to tell.' His glacier-blue eyes shone down at her as she smiled at him.

Another figure came racing over the snow and Saga laughed with delight. 'Dag!'

'Did you miss me?' He grinned back at her, coming to a stop just in front of her, where he paused awkwardly. His nose was pink, his oil-black hair spilling down, his hat still too big for him. Saga pounced on him to give him a fierce hug as he weakly protested. 'Did you see that dragon?' he asked. 'Do you think it would let us ride it?' His mouth fell open as Canute's scales shimmered back into his skin and he lost his tail.

Saga giggled. 'Probably not, but you could ask.' She introduced Dag to Ruvsá and Canute before her afi led her away to where their Jarl was having a serious discussion with Unn and Leif and several other people about what had happened and what was to be done next. Unn was standing close to another woman with short blue braids, who Saga guessed was her partner, Frida. The two women were bright with happiness, their little glances at each other shining with affection.

'I commend you, young Saga,' the Jarl told her. 'If it wasn't for you, this story could have had a very different ending.' Though his tone was solemn, his eyes were kind and Saga suddenly had a rush of relief that her part in all of this was done.

'Does that mean we can go home now?' she asked.

CHAPTER THIRTY-EIGHT
HOME AT LAST

After the Jarl of Saga's village and a couple of other local leaders in the North, including that of the Sámi, had addressed the sorcerers, decisions were swiftly made. Unn and Frida were to remain in the ice castle with the Jarl and Rollo as the four of them investigated which of the sorcerers had been involved with Baldr's terrible plot. Then they would work out what needed to happen next. The Fifth Winter Contest had been officially called off. By this point, Saga was feeling the after-effects of using too much magic and then pushing through to be reunited with her friends and Afi. She couldn't stand straight.

'Sit down,' Ruvsá told her, finding her a comfortable spot on the sorcerers' sledge as everyone made preparations to leave. It had been decided that they would travel home on the magical sledge, which was a relief after the freezing, stormy crossing the contestants had endured on their voyage to the Far North. But nobody was more relieved than Canute. 'I'll never have to sail across a sea again,' he said, sighing happily, glazed over like honey.

Saga lay there, a contented smile on her face as she listened to Dag and Canute exchange stories of fighting mountain trolls, with Ruvsá and Bjørn nestled either side of her, Ruvsá interrupting Canute's stories when they grew too far-fetched. Her afi gently wrapped a thick fur round her, tucking her in until she couldn't feel the freezing air nip any more.

'She did use the ice crystal. My mother,' Saga told him. 'All this time I was afraid of the magic inside me, but it was never the magic inside my mother that killed her.'

Afi hesitated, then showed Saga the hilt of his sword. He tapped the spent ice crystal embedded there. 'No, it was this one. If I had known that was where your fear came from, I would have told you a long time ago.'

Saga stretched out a hand, touching the dull gemstone. All this time, the answer had been right in front of her. 'I thought you told me that you used this in battle?'

'I never said it was my battle,' Afi said softly. 'I kept it to honour her. To remind me what is most important in life: protecting my loved ones. Protecting you.'

Saga smiled. 'I faced my fears and used the runes to try to find you,' she mumbled sleepily to him. 'Are you proud of me?'

'I am always proud of you,' Afi told her. 'Whether you fight off a hundred trolls single-handedly or make an exceptionally delicious stew, I am never not proud of you. You're my guiding star, Saga.' His voice turned hoarse. 'You light my world. But you've used a lot of magic today so now you need to rest. Sleep.'

And Saga finally closed her eyes.

When she woke, the sledge was flying over a forest.

'We crossed the sea last night; we should be home soon,' her afi told her, passing her a big bowl of porridge. He'd decorated it with hazelnuts and berries and thick cream until it looked like a bear's face and Saga smiled almost not wanting to eat it.

Until a real bear paw dived in before she could catch it.

'Bjørn!'

Her afi chortled. 'I see some things haven't changed.'

It wasn't long before Saga's friends woke up too and then Torben and Fenrir began the task of flying the sledge to different places to take everyone home. The shieldmaidens had disappeared during the night and Saga was disappointed that they hadn't said goodbye, but Torben shrugged, telling her, 'They like to be mysterious like that.' Then he roared a laugh and ruffled her hair. 'That was quite some battle you started back there. You let me know when you're ready for your first voyage further afield.'

Canute was taken to a large village inland, to the east. It was ringed by jagged mountains and a frozen river sliced through it. No sooner had they landed the sledge than his parents came running out.

'We should never have let you go,' his father told him as Canute vanished between his parents' hug.

'We'll never let you forget just how special you are again,' his mother added. Canute had turned pink by the time he waved goodbye to the sledge.

Then they soared to a snowy valley where smoke curled up from the pointed tips of *lávvus*, and a herd of reindeer, hundreds strong, roamed beneath the starlight. The moment the sledge stopped, a white reindeer came lolloping out of the herd, calling excitedly.

'Snowflake!' Ruvsá hopped from the sledge, running over to her reindeer. From one of the *lávvus*, three older boys emerged, who all surrounded Ruvsá, jostling each other out of the way as they each competed to talk to her first. A woman that looked identical to Ruvsá came running then, folding her daughter into her arms as she sobbed into her hair.

After giving them a few moments to themselves, Saga wandered over. 'I told you she wouldn't be cross.' Saga nudged Ruvsá affectionately.

Ruvsá was glowing. 'I guess not.' Her smile faded a little. 'We're just over the fjords,' she told Saga.

'Less than a day's journey,' Saga said back.

'Do you promise that we'll see each other again soon?' Ruvsá's eyebrows bunched together in concern. '*Very* soon?'

Saga squeezed Ruvsá's hands in hers. 'Wild mountain trolls couldn't stop me,' she teased.

There were a few more stops along the way, the raiders leaping off the sledge as they hurried back to their families, the captured villagers rushing home once more. Leif's wife eagerly scooped up their young children as her husband waved farewell to the sledge, already soaring on to their next stop.

And there, at last, nestled between great curving fjords, sat their village. It was bathed in blue light, the first real light Saga had seen since she'd left. There had never been a lovelier sight. Soon, they would celebrate Jul, and then the sun would begin to rise above the horizon once more, bringing spring to their valley.

Afi rested a hand on Saga's shoulder. 'Take it all in,' he said kindly as Saga wiped a sleeve over her eyes. 'There's nothing like that first glimpse of home after a long journey.'

'Your grandfather's a wise man.' Torben nodded sagely, stroking his sparse beard as he glanced at Afi's neatly braided beard. Saga suppressed a giggle. 'The harder and more dangerous the journey, the sweeter the return.' Torben suddenly slammed a hand on to his shield, making Saga jump. 'Now, you'll need one of these before I take you on your first raid –'

At that, Afi hurried Saga off the sledge.

Bjørn ambled behind them with Dag, and their friends and neighbours followed, exclaiming with delight at seeing their little village again. Soon fires were puffing out of longhouses and lanterns were lit along the coast, making their village cosy and twinkling once more.

'Let's get our fire lit –' Afi said, rubbing his hands together – 'and see what we can take to the feast tonight.'

But when Saga threw open the door to their longhouse, someone was already standing there.

'It's about time you returned.' The seer peered at Saga with her milky eyes. Her cat-fur hat was discarded on the table and a stew was bubbling away in the cauldron over the fire, filling the longhouse with comforting warmth.

Afi shucked off his furs, eyeing the seer warily. 'Last time you visited, you had foreseen a prophecy,' he grunted, helping Saga remove her ice-encrusted boots. 'Well, Saga did what you trusted her to do and now that her destiny is hers, I'd thank you to kindly leave it alone.'

Saga's heart thumped. She'd always known her afi was proud that she'd had a magical destiny, but it was even better to discover that he was proud of her without one too.

The seer gave a raspy chuckle that sounded like rustling leaves. 'Actually, Saga's destiny has always been her own.' She stirred the stew, ignoring the baffled looks Saga and her afi exchanged.

Bjørn huffed, stretching out before the fire and promptly falling asleep.

'But you said that I would dream magic and that I held the fate of the North in my hands,' Saga protested.

The seer gestured with a gnarled hand. 'Well, the first part was true but the second was slightly, er, *embellished*.'

'How embellished?' Afi's eyes flashed with anger.

'Oh, completely.' The seer chuckled again. 'We seers saw what was coming up in the Far North and so we searched through the threads of time and fate until we found people powerful enough to resolve the impending danger before it turned to doom and the gods got involved.' She shook her head. 'That *never* bodes well.'

Saga sat down heavily. 'So there was never a prophecy about me in the first place?'

'Not at all!' The seer started ladling out bowls of stew. Afi looked stunned. 'We merely needed a hero, and I chose Saga, trusting that if she believed she was specially chosen, if she believed in herself, she could save us all. And so she did.' The seer handed them each a bowl of stew and picked up her staff, making towards the door.

'So, I'm not special?' Saga asked.

The seer hesitated, light shining through the valleys and cracks on her face. 'Oh, you're a gemstone among rocks, dear. It is no small feat to believe in yourself, let alone march up to the Far North and battle against an entire ice castle filled with sorcerers, frost giants and mountain trolls.' She winked. 'But as for what made me choose you, well, that reason is at this very moment snoring in front of the fire.'

Saga and Afi's gaze fell on Bjørn, happily asleep, his paws twitching as he chased rabbits in his dreams.

'What you share with that bear is one of the most special things about you. It is why I chose you above the others; I knew that when the time came for you to face the fate I had chosen for you, you would not be alone. For you will never be alone, Saga. Bjørn is your guardian spirit in bear-form, and you are destined to tread your path together.'

Saga smiled at Bjørn. 'Good,' she whispered.

'Now enjoy your stew, and fear not, there are no mushrooms in it.' The seer pulled on her cat-fur hat and left, the longhouse door banging shut behind her.

Saga looked at her afi, who suddenly roared with laughter. 'Well, that was a surprise,' he admitted, picking up his bowl of stew and giving it a good sniff. 'She's a fine cook, though,' he added, finding two spoons and passing one to Saga. 'Now, come and sit beside the fire with me. I want to hear every one of your stories before you tell them at the feast later.'

Outside the longhouse, the Northern Lights danced more brightly than they had in an age, and when Saga peeked out of the door at them, her smile was every bit as bright. She was back home, with her afi, where they belonged. Her future stretched out before her, carefree and entirely her own.

Saga curled up next to the fire where Bjørn slumbered, her bowl of stew warming her hands, her afi listening as she started to weave her stories into a familiar pattern that she would tell again and again: 'I rode my bear to the Far North, over the tundra, guided by the stars and a crafty seer who meddled with my fate . . .'

ACKNOWLEDGEMENTS

The Girl who Dreamed in Magic is a magical love letter to my favourite country I've ever visited: Norway. I adored writing this book, but like any good Viking voyage, I did not sail alone!

Thank you to my wonderful agent, Thérèse Coen, for everything, and to Emma Jones and Naomi Colthurst for pushing this boat out from harbour. Huge, bear-shaped thanks to my editor Lowri Ribbons for being brilliant and making this journey so enjoyable.

My gratitude and endless appreciation to the whole Puffin team, including: Shreeta Shah, Chessanie Vincent, Arabella Jones, Louisa Hunter, Toni Budden, Kat Baker,

Acknowledgements

Sam Stanton-Stewart, Mary O'Riordan and Leena Lane.

A special thanks to Nakul P., who illustrated a cover every bit as magical as Saga's dreams!

Thank you to all the book bloggers, bookstagrammers, booktokkers, booktubers and booksellers who champion my books, especially Waterstones Nottingham and West Bridgford, and Wonderland Bookshop – I wish I could give you all a horn of magical ice crystals!

Sending sparkly thank-yous to the authors who so kindly said such nice things about this book, and to all my author friends, who I adore as much as Bjørn loves honey.

An entire ice castle of thanks must go to my family and friends, who support me and are always there for me, especially my husband, Michael Brothwood, who makes me happy every day. And to Dziadzio, who inspired a lot of Saga's afi. I miss you telling me stories but they, and you, live on in my heart.

Finally, thank you everyone who has picked up this book and joined me for this voyage; I hope you enjoyed your adventure with Saga and Bjørn!